DREAMS OF THE SPACE AGE

Ian Sales

Whippleshield Books
www.whippleshieldbooks.com
UK

Published by Whippleshield Books
www.whippleshieldbooks.com

ISBN 978-0-9931417-7-5 (limited)
ISBN 978-0-9931417-8-2 (paper)
ISBN 978-0-9931417-9-9 (ebook)

Edited by Jim Steel
Cover by Kay Sales

CONTENTS

INTRODUCTION

I couldn't have written these stories in this book. For a start, I'm not nearly as good, as *rigorous*, a writer as Ian Sales. Also, the research would kill me.

Sales has chosen a strange time in our history and set out to colonise it. It was a time of great optimism and endeavour, a time of heroes and legends, a time we perhaps don't really understand very well at all. I remember sitting in my grandparents' living room in Prestwick on July 20 1969 and watching the grainy television images of a man standing on the Moon and it seemed the pinnacle of human achievement, but that was forty-seven years ago and in a lot of ways, it seems to me, the optimism and endeavour have evaporated. We haven't been back to the Moon since 1972, and perhaps familiarity with space flight has bred, not contempt exactly, but a sense of *so what*?

The Space Age was a long time ago. From this distance, it seems rather primitive, quaint almost. As much a part of the past as the Summer of Love. It's a period which, it seems to me, science fiction doesn't talk about any more. We're told that the Space Age began with the launch of Sputnik 1 in 1957 and continues to this day, but when we use the term what we really mean is the age which ended on December 19, 1972, with the return to Earth of Apollo 17's Command Module.

Apollo 17's crew, Eugene Cernan, Harrison Schmitt and Ronald Evans, were the last men to visit the Moon, and in the intervening years we've only travelled a fraction of the distance from the home world. The optimism, the *will*, which took us to the Moon seems to have deserted us. The Space Age is over. What we're left with is space probes and a vague *intention*.

But for Ian Sales, this is territory rich with possibility. I remember sitting in the lobby of the Radisson Edwardian at Heathrow at the 2012 EasterCon and reading *Adrift on the Sea of Rains*, the first part of his Apollo Quartet, and being utterly knocked out by it. Each of the subsequent parts of the Quartet has told a complex story in the context of the Apollo and Gemini and Mercury space programmes, each of them deeply-imagined alternate worlds, building into what I think, personally, is one of the most significant achievements of British science fiction for quite a long time.

The stories in this book come, if not from the same universes as the worlds of the Apollo Quartet, then from their immediate neighbours. Sales takes the nuts and bolts of the Space Race—and they are frighteningly primitive nuts and bolts—and imagines an alternate history where the first American in space is a boxer, where *Voyager I* is a manned space probe, and Yuri Gargarin becomes the first man on Mars in an adventure which is eerily familiar...

These stories are densely-researched, and the research reveals just how insanely *dangerous* space travel is. It's a fiction of fuel-to-weight ratios, impenetrable acronyms, sweat-stained spacesuits, delta-v, Lunar Modules with hulls so thin a four-year-old could poke holes in them with a screwdriver.

At the same time, Sales has a wonderful eye for period detail. The final novel in the Apollo Quartet, *All That Outer Space Allows*, is a fabulous recreation of the late 1960s/early1970s, as is 'The Spaceman and the Moon Girl' in this collection.

Finally, these are simply great stories, crisply written and without an ounce of fat on them. Ian Sales is very, very good at what he does, and we have to hope that he keeps on doing it.

Oh, and one bit of advice when you read Ian Sales. Don't skip the footnotes.

Dave Hutchinson

BARKER

B arker is doing reps on the speed bag, fists pumping, keeping to the rhythm, the bag's a blur but he's not seeing it. There are others exercising in the gym, but he's filtered out their noise. He's focused on the bag, on the metronome thudding of his fists, on the impact of his knuckles on the smooth leather, on the sense of orderliness and control it gives him.

A voice by him says loudly, "Hey! Barker!"

It's Al the trainer. Barker slows his punching and then drops his hands. It's a moment before his attention's on Al.

"There's a coupla rocket scientists here wanna talk to you."

Barker looks over at the gym entrance and sees a pair of suits. One is tall and skinny, carrying the kind of doleful expression that means he just put his ma in the ground. The other is short, heavy, with a head like a potato and thinning black hair greased back. Black suits, white shirts, black ties.

"What they want?" he asks Al, still watching the suits.

"Talk to you." Al shrugs, sticks his stogie back in his mouth and shuffles away.

With Al's departure the two suits approach. "We're not rocket scientists," says the tall one, "but we work at Huntsville, at the Redstone Arsenal. That's where we have all the missiles and rockets, we're just... *staff*."

"So?" says Barker. Whatever they are, he can't see why they want him. He's just an Irish bantamweight, five foot six in his stockinged feet. He's no rocket scientist.

The short fat one speaks: "How would you like to be the most famous man in America? In the world, even?"

Barker never made it to the big time. He had the edge once, but it's been blunted by too many gloved fists, by the pummelling he's taken in twenty years of boxing. The scars are written on his face, across his chest and shoulders. He's proud he never threw a fight, not even for money; but integrity wins no matches.

"We want to make you the most famous man in the world," the tall one repeats. "You know the Russkies put that Sputnik up last year? Well, we're going to do better. We're going to put a man up there. And we want him to talk to the world from space."

Barker clenches his fists. He's thinking and he needs the physicality of his hands to do it, he needs to feel the bandages tight across them, the stiffness in the knuckles. He needs to feel the years of abuse he's given them. It reminds him what he is and what he's done; and when he thinks, he needs to know that.

"You want to put me up there?" he asks. He remembers Sputnik, he remembers the headlines. Some little silver ball the Soviets shot up in space on a rocket. The papers said the A-bombs would follow soon after, but it's not happened yet. There was a show about it on the TV. From memories of its crude cartoon he pictures the Earth and in orbit about it the Russian satellite.

Suspicion settles on him. "Why me?"

"We need someone in the peak of physical fitness," says short fat suit. "And, well, small; we need someone small. The rocket can only lift so much weight."

"I ain't smart," Barker replies.

"Not a problem," tall skinny suit says. "It's real simple, and we'll train you so you know what to do."

"Am I the first?"

"What?"

"Am I," repeats Barker, "the first guy you asked?"

There's a moment of silence. Tall suit says: "Ah. No."

"We asked a few before you, yes," adds short suit.

"They all said no." Barker can see from their faces he's right. "So when?"

The suits look at each other. "We want to launch December," says the tall one.

Barker has a couple of fights in the next few weeks, but he can pull out of them. His career's been in the toilet for years. If he does this, he won't ever need to box again. He can put up his hands. The dull pain will always be there— he's never going to lose that memento—but at least he'll not have to bite back the agony after they've taken and given a beating. Every time he rises to his feet from that stool in the corner, he thinks maybe this is the last time, maybe he'll come to on his back and something won't work any more. Maybe they'll have to take him away on a stretcher.

"Yeah," he says. "Yeah." He nods. "I'll do it." He bangs his taped hands together knuckles to knuckles, and he thinks maybe some things aren't fated after all.

☆

Dr Wernher von Braun is not happy. "A man is not a fruit fly," he insists. "In 1942, I sent up fruit flies; but this is a man! We are not ready."

Ten years in the US, and his German accent still weighs down his words with Teutonic gravitas. A big man, well-fed like a farmer, though he'd be insulted if it were said. He turns his back on Major David Simons and gazes out of the window at White Sands. It is not the cold wind-whipped Baltic of Peenemünde he sees, but a dry yellow sea of sand and scrub.

"You wanted to put a monkey up, so what's the difference?" asks General Bernard Schriever.

As commander of the Ballistic Missiles Division of the US Air Force, this project is Schriever's. He doesn't really want von Braun involved, he doesn't like it one bit. He despises the Operation Paperclip scientists. As a German who emigrated before Hitler's evil regime, he has nothing but contempt for their complicity. And he hates them more because he knows his country needs the Nazis.

"A monkey is not a man also," says von Braun.

Simons speaks up, "I thought we already had some test pilots picked out. If we're not going to use them, I don't see why we have to use this boxer guy."

None reply to Simons' complaint—they know he himself wants to go. In Project Manhigh, he's come closer to space than anyone, over 100,000 feet above the earth in a balloon. They also know President Eisenhower isn't interested in space, and refuses to let test pilots be involved. They will be needed if war breaks out with the Soviets.

"He's expendable," Schriever says. "He's also small."

"A monkey is expendable," retorts von Braun. "And smaller also."

"We've been through this," Schriever says. "Ike is going to kill the project if we don't give him something. It's gotta make the Russkies sit up and take notice. And a guy up in orbit, talking to the world, is better than any damn bleep-bleep-bleep or monkey pressing buttons."

"Ach," says von Braun. He turns back from the window. His gaze drifts to the model of the Redstone rocket on his desk and it's clear he's made up his mind.

Schriever swears and turns away in disgust. Von Braun doth protest too much—and then he folds like a poker player with a hand full of nothing.

But at least he's going to give the project his rocket.

☆

Barker watches as the doctor straps his hand down onto a desk. All these medical tests. The blood test, the urine test—these he can understand. But semen? The enema?

It occurs to him these doctors don't know what they're doing. There's no way they can know. No one's ever been up in outer space, they don't know what it'd do to a man. Barker guesses he's going to find out. But at least these doctors covered their own asses with all these dumb tests.

The doctor is holding a heavy steel needle attached to a wire. Barker eyes it with suspicion. The doctor slams the needle down into Barker's hand, just by his thumb joint. Barker yelps, swears a blue streak and tries to pull his hand away.

"Keep still," the doctor says. He looks over Barker's head at the orderly by the door.

Fool, thinks Barker. The orderly may be built like Rocky Marciano, but he's no boxer. One punch to the jaw and he'll break like a cheap vase.

There's some equipment on a bench nearby. The doctor twists a knob, and Barker's hand clenches.

Barker makes his living from his hands and this has him sweating, a cold sweat in the small of his back that drips down his spine. His hand... he's not doing it himself, he's not telling his hand to clench, he's not making it form a fist, like when he throws those knuckles into a man's face or gut. His fists are dangerous weapons, *his* dangerous weapons. They're not for someone else to use.

"Take that goddamn thing offa me," he yells. He reaches for the straps securing his hand to the desk.

His pinned hand clenches and unclenches.

The orderly lumbers forward and grabs Barker's shoulders.

"Get it offa me," Barker bellows.

He's scared now. His hand is no longer his, it's like his fight has been snatched from him. He's just a goddamn puppet and the doctor is pulling the strings.

Moments later, the doctor removes the needle and unstraps Barker's hand. The orderly is out cold on the floor. Barker doesn't remember clocking him, but he can still feel the impact in the knuckles of his free hand.

He sits there, his hands held up in front of him; he clenches and unclenches them, and he knows he's doing it himself. He forms fists and practices a couple of quick jabs. He bangs his knuckles together. He feels less fearful now, he has his fists back. He knows their topography intimately, the history attached to every misshapen peak and valley of his knuckles. His resumé is written there on his hands, and it is *his*. Not theirs, not some goddamn doctor's, not these goddamn rocket scientists.

"Never again," he warns the doctor. "Not that one. *Never.*"

☆

Barker is sitting in his silver pressure suit while the technician goes off to find a replacement glove. He's not thinking. He's good at not thinking, and when it comes to this thing he's signed up for, his mind shies away from the consequences. They showed him films of earlier rocket launches. They all blew up. Von Braun, who either patronises him or blinds him with rocket science, says he can't guarantee Barker's rocket won't explode on launch. So Barker doesn't think about it. He blanks his mind. He says nothing to the psychologist they got watching him. He tells no one that he lies awake at night in a cold sweat, worse than the night before a big fight.

Some guy pokes his head into the room, then steps

inside. He's wearing a suit, but he looks military. Short hair, round face. He nods at Barker, then stands there saying nothing.

"I know you?" Barker asks.

The guy shakes his head. "I'm a test pilot," he says.

"Right," replies Barker without much enthusiasm.

"I wanted to say, have a good flight," the test pilot says.

"You one of them that volunteered for this?"

"I was selected for the 'Man In Space Soonest' programme last year."

He doesn't say much this test pilot, he doesn't move much either. It's like he's guarding every heartbeat. Barker sits and waits out his scrutiny. He's done this before, at the weighing-in, eyeing up the other guy, spotting his weaknesses, looking for the guy's secret, what he's going to pull out when they're both swaying on their feet from exhaustion. Maybe this test pilot is doing the same, maybe he thinks he gets to go if Barker takes a dive.

"So what's your name?" asks Barker.

"Neil Armstrong."

"Hey, maybe you get to be first at something else instead," says Barker.

Armstrong stops in the doorway and looks back at Barker in his silver monkey suit. He nods like he just deep-down knows that's going to happen one day, and then he walks away.

They decided to base the spacecraft on the Manhigh II capsule. Simons argued for it and he's still angling to be the man in it, the *astronaut*. Barker doesn't care. The capsule is small, he knew that already. Else they wouldn't have picked him, a bantamweight boxer. All week there's been a line of test pilots flying in to Huntsville to come look at him—Armstrong was just the first. Barker doesn't know where they come from, he doesn't care where they come from.

They look at him, they say he's no pilot. Then they go away.

But Barker will be *first*, and he sees the pain of that on their faces as they gaze at him. They've got some firsts already, some of them—fastest, highest; records broken every week. He hears they got this rocket plane they're going to build that'll go all the way up to the edge of space.

But not into orbit.

That's where Barker's going, and by now he knows exactly what that means. He's going to be 150 miles up, circling the earth, looking down on the world. He's going to be on top for the first time in his life, he's going to be a winner, a big shot winner, the biggest in the world. When he focuses on that, then he doesn't care these rocket scientists have no idea what they're doing.

They have him squeezed into a mock-up of the capsule and they make him flick switches. It's dumb, it's like a monkey could do it. He has to remember which ones to flick but it's all written down. He'll have the list with him when he goes up.

They put him in a centrifuge and next thing he knows he's like some heavyweight, and he laughs like he can take down Floyd Patterson and Rocky Marciano both with one blow. The technician asks him to flick some more switches, and he lifts his fists of stone and does as he's told. Each breath is a chore but he feels like a man of steel, he knows he can punch holes in walls with these hands like rock.

They throw him out of an airplane with a parachute on his back. Simons tells him a captain he knows almost died a week before when he jumped from a balloon at 76,000 feet. His stabilizer chute caught round his neck and set him spinning. It knocked him cold. Simons is trying to scare Barker, they both know it. But Barker's career is facing down fear and he'll never show to another man what frightens him.

Besides, Kittinger lived: his main chute opened automatically at 10,000 feet.

Simons leaves the project soon after. It's getting close to

the launch date, and now they got to make sure the rocket works and doesn't blow up on the pad. There's tests for the capsule, for the electronic and radio stuff, for the rocket-engine and fuel-pumps. Barker has never been anything but a passenger, but now he's like nothing. They don't ask him what he thinks, they don't tell him what they're doing—he's just a lump of meat to them. He knows what he's got to do—his head has taken plenty of beatings in twenty years, bits of it don't work as well as they should, but he's still smarter than a monkey. Some say he's the most fallible component in the project, like they expect him to fail; but they're testing all those valves and pumps and switches and dials like they don't expect them to work either.

☆

Two hours he's spent on his back in this capsule, two hours staring up at switches and dials. He doesn't know what most of them do, he doesn't much care. Whatever he has to press or flick is written down in the list strapped to his thigh. He can hear chatter on the radio but he understands little of it. Delays, technical stuff, little things which mean they can't light this candle just yet. Barker waits patiently, not thinking.

They tell him they have go for launch. He says he's been go since whenever, this is the longest he ever spent awake on his back. The countdown enters the last minute. Time's been elastic since they crammed him into this flying closet. It feels like days he's been here, he's got no window to see the minutes pass.

"Ten... nine... eight...," says the guy in Mission Control.

It's like when Barker's opponent is out for the count, flat on the mat. The seconds stretch like taffy and he thinks the guy's eyes are going to pop open, he's going to struggle to his feet, and Barker is going to have to hit him again and again and again.

"... three... two... one. We have lift-off."

Something starts to shake under Barker. He can hear a low mumble, but it's far away, in another building. The capsule starts to shake, the dials in front of him blur.

Now he can feel movement—he's going up. Everything's rattling and vibrating, the noise is getting louder and louder. He grins up at the stars above him. Something is sat on his chest, it's like the centrifuge, and the grin becomes a laugh and he remembers having fists of stone.

This shaking is bad, but his brain has been bounced around so many times inside his skull it's got callouses, so he rides through it.

Everything abruptly stops.

Barker is thrown forward against his straps. He grunts, it hurts it's so unexpected. There's a moment of stillness, a heavenly calm, and he feels like maybe he's died. He even feels a lightness, his ass rising up from his seat.

Then he's slammed back down as the second stage ignites, and he knows he's got more time yet to struggle through. The ride is smoother now, the sound has whispered away, he feels only a dim rumble through his seat.

They should, he thinks, have given him a goddamn window.

☆

Barker can feel his kneecaps drying out and they begin to hurt. He can't move his legs—they're strapped in because there's no leg-room. He massages his knees with his hands but it doesn't help. It's getting warm. A bead of sweat rolls down his forehead, he can feel it on his brow. He tries to shake his head, but can only manage an inch or two either way in the helmet. He checks the clock on the instrument panel. Another fifteen minutes and he'll be over the continental United States. That's when he gets to give the speech.

The words he will speak are taped to the instrument

panel beside the clock. Barker thinks he's going to sound like a phoney. He doesn't speak like that, he says "yeah" and "goddamn", and he's never used a five-dollar word in his life. But they got to look good for the Russkies, for the world, so they've given him some fancy speech to read out.

It's getting warmer. There's no temperature gauge on the instrument panel, but he can feel it. He lifts a hand to wipe his forehead and his glove bangs against the visor of his space helmet. He swears. A drop of sweat slides down his nose; one eye starts to smart.

Quarter of an hour later, Barker is soaked. He can feel sweat dribbling down his calves, down his back. He blinks repeatedly to clear the salt from his eyes. He can even feel his goddamn ankles sweating. It's getting hard to breathe, the air piped into his pressure suit is so hot. He swears, but the heat has sapped his energy and he can't get any real venom into the words.

There is a crackle in his headphones, and then a voice: "Adam 1, Adam 1, this is Cape. Do you read? Over."

Barker grunts. He pulls in a breath, and then replies: "Goddammit, you bastards. It's like a goddamn oven in here."

"Roger. Read you loud and clear. Nix on the profanities, Adam 1. This is being broadcast. Do you have something you want to say?"

They want him to read his speech to the world. He's having trouble breathing, he'll never get out those fancy words. But he'll not hit the mat without a fight, he owes them that much, he owes *himself* that much. They put him up here to give the speech, so that's what he'll do. He pulls in a ragged lungful of air. The pain makes him gasp but he forges ahead:

"This is Adam 1 in orbit about the Earth."

He breaks off. He's panting now, he can feel his strength draining out through his legs and feet, as if it belonged to the Earth and were returning to it.

"I can't do it," he says. "Goddamn."

"What's the problem, Adam 1?" asks Cape.

"How long... you keeping... me... up here?" Barker demands. There's no gravity in orbit but he still doesn't have the strength to move.

"Three more orbits, Adam 1. About another four and one half hours."

"I can't last that goddamn long."

"We've got, ah, a glitch in the telemetry. You said it's getting hot in the capsule?"

Barker tries to laugh. This is the worst fight he's ever fought, worse than any fight he can imagine. He's taking a beating. "It *is* hot, you goddamn pencil-necks," he tells them. One of the test pilots gave him that phrase: pencil-necks. It fits.

"Roger that. We think maybe some insulation came off the capsule during launch. The temperature control system wasn't designed to cope with that eventuality. It's going to be rough, Adam 1, but we calculate we can bring you down in another two orbits."

It's getting hotter. He can barely breathe now. This *eventuality* is killing him. He's sucking in air through compressed lips and it's burning his throat. His skin is slick with sweat and he's sliding about inside his pressure suit. "No!" he says, forcing out the syllable and then letting out a yell at the pain in his lungs.

He knows he's a dead man. Another two goes around. He won't make it. He pulls in a deep scorching breath. It might be his last.

"You've goddamn killed me," he yells. "Goddamn you, you goddamn pencil-necks. You've killed me, you've goddamn killed me."

He roars one last time as his sight begins to dim.

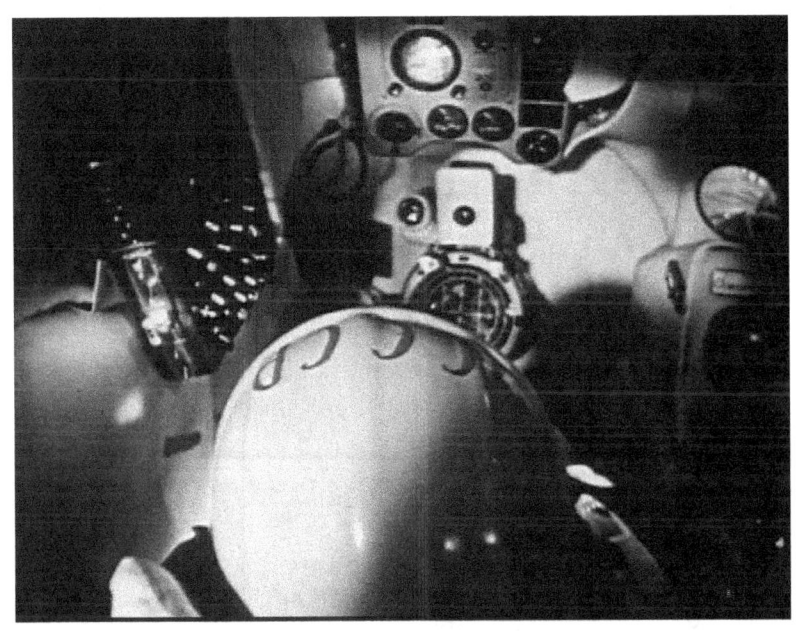

FAITH

12 April 1961

At 7,000 metres, a deafening bang fills the capsule, and bright light pours in from above his head. The steel-grey of the SIS-1-3KA control panel, with its navigation globe of the earth, glows as if minted in silver. He has only a moment to remark on this before he is catapulted head-first through the hatch. His world, close and spherical and dimly-lit, suddenly expands to limitless white. The capsule, a charred and blackened sphere, drops away from him, shrinking as it falls into an ocean of haze. Vostok 1, his *sharik*, his "little ball", he feels deserves a salute for its service, and so he raises a hand in farewell. It kept him free from harm; it protected him from the cold vacuum of space and the fiery inferno of re-entry.

He unbuckles his harness and separates from his

ejection-seat. For several minutes, they fall together, separated only by a metre or two. Now he feels a deep sadness at being parted from his chair, and reaches out but it is too far away to touch. They have gone where no man has gone before, he and that chair. They have circled the earth and looked down upon it from a height never before reached. The chair is a part of him: it held him safely, securely, in its embrace; and he rues his need to discard it.

They drift apart as they fall. He rolls over, his back to the chair. The sky in every direction is a blue so pale it is white. There are no clouds and no horizon. He falls through a world of nothing. He cannot see the ground below, he cannot see the sun above him.

His parachute is set to deploy automatically at 2,500 metres. At the speed he is falling, surely he should reach that point soon. He swings out his arms and rolls onto his front. His helmet keeps the rushing air from his face. He has made parachute jumps many times before, but this freefall reminds him of his hour in space. Though he had been strapped into his ejection-seat, he had watched in amazement as his hands had drifted of their own accord up before his face. He had felt a lightness in his being, as if he were being called to heaven. I feel splendid, very well, very well, very well, he had told the ground station at Khabarovsk.

Oh, he had felt so very well. Not only privileged, but *chosen*. Closer to God and His dominion. He had experienced such joy, to see the world as God must, to gaze down upon Mother Russia, and the other nations of the world. To know everyone was within his all-encompassing view. A great magnanimity had filled him, made of him a vessel of heavenly light and joy, and he knew the world had changed irrevocably.

Even now, as he falls toward his meeting with the black earth of home, toward his meeting with destiny, he still feels the touch of God. He holds out his arms, as if to embrace the world below him. Yet still he can see nothing, only this limitless haze, this pale white sea of pearlescent light.

It has been more than ten minutes. Why has his chute not deployed? Why has he not reached the ground? Where is his ejection-seat?

He falls alone; he falls forever.

16 May 1963

The capsule hangs beneath the red-and-white-striped main chute and swings heavily in an abbreviated circle. Within, the astronaut lies on his back, sweating inside his silver pressure suit. The cabin temperature has been rising since the spacecraft suffered a total power failure on the nineteenth orbit. The heat spiked during re-entry, and he thought he might black out. Only the radio and the television camera still function. As he piloted the spacecraft from orbit, he suffered in silence, waving once at the television camera on the instrument panel, just to let them know he was in control, he was *flying* his spacecraft. But now he has deployed the chute, and he lies there and waits, knowing soon that his spacecraft will hit the water at thirty-two feet per second. But he does not know when and he is no longer controlling the spacecraft. Throughout the mission, he has presented his usual laconic self, though it has taken an effort of will to place his safety, his survival, in the hands of pencil-necks and rocket scientists.

He keeps his face carefully blank, perhaps even the hint of a smile. He had seen a demonstration of the television before launch, and the picture quality was not very good. He imagines himself a ghost, a blurred figure of white and grey and black seeming to only just inhabit the television screen. The thought prompts another thumbs-up towards the camera.

Though he has remained tensed and expectant for the past ten minutes, splashdown still takes him by surprise.

The capsule hits the water, sinks a dozen feet, and then then bobs back up sickeningly. Now he is rocking in the swell. He reaches up, unlatches and pulls off his helmet. The interior of the spacecraft is stifling hot, and there is sweat plastered across his brow, but his head still feels a little cooler without the enclosing helmet. He is tempted to blow the hatch, but he remembers only too well what happened to Gus when he did that. He knows some of the others don't like him much, so he has no plans to make himself a target of jokes and sneers by sinking Faith 7.

If he has figured his re-entry correctly, he should be less than ten miles from the USS Kearsage. He can't see anything through the capsule's window but clear blue Pacific sky.

He tells Hawaii he's doing fine, and then radios the aircraft carrier for permission to come aboard. Scott told him this was the correct protocol. They tell him a helicopter is on its way to drop a flotation collar. He wonders if he'll see the aircraft—the window covers only a narrow arc of sky. He should at least hear the whup-whup of its rotor.

He waits patiently. Whenever someone speaks to him on the radio, he replies. But his famous laconism is sorely tested as the minutes stretch by. The capsule is like a bathtub full of boiled air and he wants out. He briefly considers climbing up through the top of the capsule as Scott had done, but elects instead to remain inside.

And then the Kearsage's captain tells him the aircraft carrier is alongside and soon he'll be lifted aboard, but he can see nothing through the window. He has not even seen the Navy frogmen who fitted the flotation collar—assuming the capsule now has such a collar. Surely they would have banged on the hatch to let him know of their arrival? He queries Hawaii, and they confirm the frogmen have done their job.

He feels a sudden and debilitating sense of loneliness, but cannot explain it. The voices on the radio provide some company, but he longs for the sight of a human face. He waves at the television camera, as if the action brings an audience into existence. And so it does, as he's told mission control are waving back at him on the screen they have there.

Now they inform him he's being swung out of the water, but he can still feel the gentle bob and swell of the ocean beneath his back. He can see no ship, no superstructure, no sheer grey wall of ship's hull. Nothing has changed.

Minutes pass. Then a voice on the radio calls his name.

Yeah? he replies.

We just opened the hatch. The capsule is empty.

You got the right spacecraft? he jokes, though he does not find the situation funny.

We can see you on the television, the voice continues. But the capsule is empty.

I'm here, damn it. He holds up a hand to the television camera.

You just put up your hand, yeah we see that. But this capsule, it says Faith 7 on the side but you're not inside. It's empty.

I damn well am inside, he snaps.

But he knows that he sits in a capsule which floats alone in a vast ocean. Were he to blow the hatch, he would be able to see to the horizon in all directions.

And all he would see was water.

3 June 1965

Everyone hears him say, It's the saddest moment of my life; and then they wait for the news that he has re-entered the Gemini 4 spacecraft and the hatch has been latched shut.

The commander leans across to the other seat, ready to help guide his crewmate into his seat and his legs into the footwell. And he waits patiently, hoping he is not going to refuse to come in, as he has been doing for the past ten

27

minutes. He's been out there twenty-three minutes now, the first American to spacewalk. It's going to be hard to get him back in, given he's already complained several times how hot and tired he is.

Then the commander notices that the gold-covered umbilical which snakes out the open hatch has vanished. Puzzled, he sits back in his seat, and then reaches up and struggles to unlatch his own hatch. Eventually he manages to open it—it has the same problem with the spring as the other hatch. He undoes his harness and pushes himself up to stand in the open hatchway.

There should be a figure in a white spacesuit floating alongside the capsule.

He can see no one.

There is the Earth beneath him, a curved plain of blue marbled with clouds. Beneath the shifting smears of white, he can see the green and brown of continents rolling past. He twists about but sees only the black heavens and stars, everywhere stars. Keeping firm grip on the lip of the hatch, he leans over the edge of the spacecraft but can see nothing there. If his crewmate had slipped his 23-foot umbilical, he would still be visible. He could not have moved so far away so soon.

His radio is still set on PUSH-TO-TALK, so he cannot speak to Mission Control unless he sits back down in his seat. Reluctantly, he pushes himself back down and fastens his harness. He says, We have a problem. I can't see him.

He's under the spacecraft? asks Capcom. If he is, he needs to get inside right now.

No, he's gone. So has the umbilical.

The radio hisses.

Did you hear me? he asks. I told him to come in, he was coming in, then he just disappeared.

What do you mean 'disappeared'? He should be tethered.

The umbilical has gone too.

It got loose? The connector disengaged? He has ten

minutes of air in a chest-pack.

He's nowhere, the commander insists. One second he was there, the next he'd gone, the umbilical had gone, like they were never there.

Another voice comes on the loop: This is no time for pranks. Is he back in the capsule?

No, he says. I keep on goddamn telling you: he's gone.

And he looks across at the seat beside him and the hatch open above it, the light of Earth shining in, a pearly white light on the empty seat. His crewmate has really gone, he's going to have to pilot this spacecraft back home alone.

He wonders if the Gemini programme can survive this setback. And he wonders at his own callousness in thinking of his crewmate's disappearance as a 'setback'.

It has changed them all, he realises; one man vanishes and the world will never be the same again.

☆

30 June 1971
A pillar of brown dust billows up suddenly into the air as the retros fire, and then the capsule hits the ground with a flat thud. The parachute collapses gracefully to one side and drapes itself across the scrubby grass. For a moment, all is still, a blackened sphere sitting in a circle of black earth. Then the vehicles and helicopters appear. A fleet of trucks and off-road vehicles race across the steppe towards the capsule. They come to a stop some two hundred metres away and people in uniform boil from doors and truckbeds.

Half a dozen technicians, soldiers crowding behind them, gather at the hatch. Quickly, they unscrew the bolts holding the hatch sealed. They are worried: there has been no word from Soyuz 11 since it entered the atmosphere. Even after the ionisation effects had ended and communication was once again possible, the crew did not answer radio calls.

The hatch is lowered carefully to the ground. Everyone

pushes forward. They all peer within. The three cosmonauts—Georgiy Timofeyevich Dobrovolsky, Vladislav Nikolayevich Volkov and Viktor Ivanovich Patsayev—are in their seats. They do not look at the open hatch, they do not move. Their faces do not change expression. They should be happy to see the ground crew, they should be smiling at having successfully completed their twenty-two days in orbit aboard Salyut. They have set a world record for the longest time spent in space.

A technician scrambles inside the capsule, though there is very little room. But still he is ignored by the cosmonauts. Dressed in blue coveralls, they remain motionless in their form-fitting seats.

They do not smile, they do not move, they do not breathe. The technician bends over Volkov, and tentatively puts his fingers to the cosmonaut's cheek. His flesh is cold, not with the chill of space but with the chill of a place from which no one ever returns. Both Patsayev and Dobrovolsky are the same. They are, the technician notices, at peace. They have not died violent deaths, but quietly and with deep courage. The technician's heart fills with pride that his country should produce such heroes, that Mother Russia should be made of men such as these.

Later, the technicians and engineers discover what had happened. There is a valve in the hatch which opens to equalise the air pressure inside the capsule as it descends to earth. During Soyuz 11's separation from Salyut, it had jammed open and all the air inside the capsule had slowly escaped.

But the valve can be closed manually—there is a handle stored beneath one of the seats. This can be attached to the valve. All it needs is nineteen turns.

Nineteen turns.

Pity Patsayev, Dobrovolsky and Volkov. All they had to do was ignore the hiss of air escaping from the spacecraft, ignore the increasing difficulty of breathing, ignore the cold seeping into the capsule, ignore the building pain in their chests, the numbness stealing into the hands and feet...

If only they had the strength to take the handle and attach it to the valve. If only they had the will to make those nineteen turns. And it would be *only* nineteen turns. Of that, they could be certain.

THE SPACEMAN AND
THE MOON GIRL

He sits with eighteen of his peers in a room at the Manned Spacecraft Center while reporters launch questions, most of which could be answered by referring to the press releases NASA has handed out; and he's wearing his best suit, it's served him well for several years, the best he can afford on his USAF captain's salary although he'd much rather be wearing a flight suit or maybe his Air Force service dress, but NASA were clear on the protocol and four of the guys are civilians anyway. So he's trying to show he has the Right Stuff coming out the wazoo, because there's not just the other guys in Group 5 but the Mercury guys and the astronaut groups NASA picked in '62, '63 and '65, and he knows he's going to be compared to them just as much as he will be to the guys sitting up here with him on the dais...

He's there in the "barrel" and his wife, she's back in New York, because this was not an assignment she could turn down, not unless she wanted bookers and editors to "forget" her face; so she's one of half a dozen models striking poses and swallowing insults from a photographer with an ego the size of the Moon because *Vogue* is doing a feature on Pierre Cardin and his Space Age designs. She thinks briefly on her husband, and maybe he's going to the Moon like the President said—and that's kind of ironic because two years before she modelled for André Courrèges' "Moon Girl" collection—but at another barked order from the photographer she's back in herself, and she's not going to forget it—the metallic silver Lurex tights are scratchy, the long vinyl gloves are sticky under the hot lights, the blue "Cardine" dress with its pattern molded into the fabric like a goddamn eggbox—they say Cardin invented the material with Union Carbide—the dress is heavy though it hangs beautifully, the black vinyl high-heeled boots are just as hot as the gloves, and the hat, or whatever the hell it is, more like a bonnet, she can feel the brim of it tight across her forehead; but at least she's not wearing the one that looks like an upturned bucket. Despite all that, she does feel kind of Space Age and she can imagine a future where she might wear these clothes while her husband goes to work in outer space.

And that night, she gets a phone call from her husband and he wants her in Houston to set up home, because NASA is all super-family and wives are wives first and nothing else second, unless they have kids, in which case they're mothers too. He's picked out a plot of land on Nassau Bay and he wants her there to find a contractor and oversee building the house while he's at the Cape training to be an astronaut. They fight. She has a career to think of, they agreed she could do this until they were ready to start a family—and she privately accepts she's delayed that start time after time—and if he can go and strap himself to a rocket and get blasted into space, she doesn't see why suddenly he has a goddamn problem with her appearing in *Vogue* and *McCall's* and *Harper's Bazaar*....

He'll win, she's known from the beginning he will win, and in defeat she belatedly realises that all along he "allowed" her this last year in New York because he was so busy with his secret project, that Mach 3 fighter jet, back at Edwards AFB. But that's all over, that's all done; and now?

Now he's an astronaut.

The house gets built but she even does that wrong, because she picks a different builder to the one used by all the other astronaut families; and now the resentment lies heavy over Nassau Bay like the oily miasma which pollutes the air from the refineries down the coast. They're the only couple with no children—and he acts like this this means they've failed in their patriotic duty, but she had no intention of ever giving up her career, she married him for love not to become a brood mare for the family name. So they build the house, she moves in and she goes to the tea parties at the Lakewood Yacht Club, and the Astronaut Wives Club's meetings, she's not the only one that had a modelling career though she was by far the most successful, and certainly the longest to resist playing the Air Force wife; but this life, this world, is stultifying, oppressive, and she wants New York back, she wants the glamour and the lights and the haute couture back.

So when she hears about the "Cape cookies" and she doesn't want to believe he's as faithless as the rest of them, she flies down there and she struts into the Holiday Inn wearing something by Paco Rabanne that was on the catwalks of Paris only a couple of years before, one of his "12 Unwearable Dresses in Contemporary Materials", but it's not unwearable now; although this particular dress is a Chip-an-Outfit kit from Mass Originals, not that she's ever going to tell anyone, and it looks goddamn Space Age. There's her husband in his blue NASA flight jacket with its flame-orange Rayon lining, looking every inch the astronaut, sitting pretty at the top of the pyramid, and so he should as they've just announced the crew for the next flight, so yes, he's *really* going to the Moon. She stands there in the doorway of the hotel bar, and all the press present turn to look at her, and she knows she looks like she just fell out of the future into Space City, where they send men into space every day. It took her weeks to make this minidress, connecting up all the little white plastic discs with metal rings, it makes faint clacking noises as she moves—how Space Age is that?—and she's wearing it over a white shift to preserve some modesty, and white pantyhose—and there sits her husband, he's in the real Space Age, he's going into space, to the Moon.

He jumps to his feet and rushes across to her, and it's all baby baby, I thought you were back home, what are you doing here; and she can see some of the guys and those women they're with are not their wives, but at least *he* is alone, at least there's no "cookie" she can see might have been his; and she's starting to feel a bit foolish, that maybe she misjudged him, maybe she put too much credence in rumours, these Original Nineteen are not the Sacred Seven after all, things have changed. But now there's photographers and this she does know how to do, so they pose and she tells them she had a sudden urge to see her husband and congratulate him, and she makes no mention of the other wives' stories about what goes on at the Cape because it's just occurred to her they're trapped back in Houston by their children, by their lives; and they envy her the freedom being childless should have given her, but up until now she's been too blind to see it.

☆

On the day, she sits on the floor before the television set in the commander's house, while behind her the other wives see to food and drinks for those present, but her husband's only the LMP so all the attention is focused on the commander's wife; but they're both in the same situation, their husbands currently inhabiting a tiny cabin with aluminium walls no thicker than a Coke can's, on a tiny world with no air, a world that can kill in a heartbeat. She's proud, thrilled and happy—they all are, they always will be, to admit to anything else would jeopardise their husbands' careers—although as he's about to set foot on the lunar surface there's not much higher he can go. She knows soon she will have to go outside with the other two wives and talk to the press, so she's chosen her outfit with care. Since Emilio Pucci designed the mission patch, she thought it fitting to wear one of his creations, not that many will realise, a silk jersey minidress in a bold print, but she's not wearing the matching leggings, the other wives nixed that, just tan pantyhose and sandals. She stopped feeling Space Age a year earlier when they announced the crew for this mission, she's not been in Space City since, and nowhere near the future, she's not even in the present—all these astronaut wives, it's like the '50s, like the '60s never happened, never mind it's now the '70s. Her husband told her, in no uncertain terms, she was an astronaut's wife and nothing else, and just maybe he can forgive her not wanting to start a family, not just yet anyhow, but she's got to fly straight and get in formation, because he's depending on her, she's his wingman. And she bit back the retorts and put her ambitions on hold and vowed to herself she's going to be "primly stable" while he flies to the Moon...

Which is where he is now, of course, backing out of the LM's hatch, bouncing down the ladder affixed to the landing leg, and now he turns to the TV camera on the LM, waves and then jumps up, propelling himself upwards using his ankles, because this A7LB spacesuit is keeping him alive but it's no picnic wearing it, with its twenty-one layers—Teflon-coated Beta Cloth, aluminized Kapton, Beta marquisette, aluminized Mylar, Dacron, Neoprene-coated nylon, nylon, Neoprene-coated nylon bladder restraint, Neoprene bladder, knit jersey laminate and Nomex comfort layer—worn over a Liquid Cooling Garment; and the polycarbonate helmet and over it the Lunar Extravehicular Visor Assembly with its gold-coated visor, all made for him at a cost of around $400,000. But if he damages it, it's going to cost him more than that, it'll cost him his life.

On the good green Earth, heart-breakingly lonely and precious in a black sky above the lunar horizon, it's late afternoon and the Texan sun beats down on Nassau Bay, the air is like a glass dish hot from the oven, and she stands outside the commander's house before the world, one of three wives. She's doing her best to be proud, thrilled and happy, though the Pucci's a little loud, but the press have decided she's "quirky" and they like that. She looks up but it's too bright and the Moon isn't visible, and she's thinking about what she's just seen on the television, what's she's just heard on the "squawk box" provided by NASA—her husband the living embodiment of American know-how, American can-do, in a place where nothing can live; and there's nothing quirky about his A7LB spacesuit.

But here in Nassau Bay, this is not the Space Age—though she has worn the label for years, clad by a succession of designers trying to create the future, she knows the real Space Age is not in her closet but on another world, a grey and lifeless world.

Once, she was a "Moon Girl"; but she knows now she'll never go to the Moon.

THE INCURABLE
IRONY OF THE MAN
WHO RODE THE
ROCKET SLED

The Gee Whiz runs on rails but it is not a train. It doesn't go anywhere: it just goes from standing still to around 200 miles per hour, and then stops. Very quickly. That's all it does, on a track two thousand feet long. It's a standard gauge railroad track, set in concrete, which runs through the desert just north of Muroc Air Force Base. The track was built in 1944 to test launch German V-1 rockets, but it's not used for that now. Now, it sends men on short journeys at high speed.

Some journeys cover more than just distance and carry more than simply passengers. Though they are undertaken by people, they are journeys of change and, with each foot they travel from their origin, the world becomes a place new and strange and different. Not all such journeys are in the interest of peace or society, not every vehicle was built for science or commerce. These 2,000-foot-long journeys for Project MX981 are military; it is a military project. With a military objective.

The sergeant stands beside the Gee Whiz, an open framework fifteen feet long and six and a half feet wide. Behind a wooden windshield is fitted a sturdy seat. At the rear of the Gee Whiz, a rack holds up to four Aerojet rocket bottles, each one capable of generating 5,000 pounds of thrust. It is another hot day, the sun beating down on the railroad tracks and their concrete bed. The sergeant takes his cigarette from his mouth, drops it and grinds it into the sand with the tip of one boot. He knows Major John P Stapp has already completed two dozen runs on this thing, and the way the major jokes about it no harm was plainly done. But this sled is going to blast the sergeant to 200 mph and then brake to a halt in under a second. He's starting to wonder why he volunteered for this project.

It's not like he's a stranger to risk. Six years ago, he was in Europe, flying over Germany as the tail-gunner in a B-17. He completed his twenty-five missions, came back home to his wife, and now the war's been over for four years and he's an air force technician at Muroc AFB. All the same, he's thinking this thing is insane and he doesn't care what the major says...

Except it's hard not to admire the "Careful Daredevil".

Stapp, with his jokes and his "rules", a strange man but well-liked—and not just because he provides free medical care to those on the base who can't afford it. He would never allow anyone to ride this rocket sled if he had not ridden it himself. And here he is now, striding toward the track, big smile on his face, sunlight turning the lenses of his spectacles into rounded squares of brightness. He swings out an arm in an expansive gesture, as if the hot shimmering desert surrounding them were some paradisiacal land and everyone present blessed to be here, and quotes his "Sunshine Law".

The major's cheer is infectious, but as soon as the sergeant steps up onto the sled his wariness returns. He settles in the aluminium seat. It is warm from the sun. Technicians strap him in securely, and help him fit his leather crash helmet. They connect up strain gauges across his chest. With a last thumbs up, the technicians retreat. The sergeant watches them go, smiles weakly in response as Stapp gives him a cheery salute, and then looks forward. There's nothing to see, just the inch-thick wooden windshield.

He hears the rocket bottles light behind him, a roar like nothing he's heard before. It doesn't even sound like it's man-made. As the Gee Whiz hurtles forward, he's pressed back into his seat and the strain forces a grunt from him. To either side, the landscape rushes past, the scrub a green blur, the desert smeared into a single strip of tan. He feels real fear, and he knows the worst is yet to come—

Here it is. The brakes engage. He's thrown forward against his straps. Red churns across the desert, a tsunami of blood. His vision closes in and...

That evening, he drives to Lancaster, fingers tapping on the steering wheel of his Mercury Eight, as the sun paints lavender and rose across the silent desert, and he's alone on the blacktop but he feels secure. The throb of the flathead V8 and the sigh of the wind sing of the world as-is and the world to-be. He barrels down Sierra Highway, through the centre of Lancaster, turns off toward his subdivision, and minutes later pulls into the driveway of his home. He sits there a moment, engine ticking as it cools, and he stares hard without seeing. Moments later, he jumps out of the car, runs lightly to the open front door, and enters the house. Donna is in the kitchen, bent over before the oven as she lifts out a baking tray. A pair of lidded saucepans sit on unlit burners. He can smell meatloaf, the air is thick with the odour of it.

And music: Peggy Lee is singing on the radio, something about mañana, mañana, mañana is soon enough for me. He strides forward, puts his hands to his wife's hips, leans forward and kisses her on the crown of her blond head. She tuts affectionately as she slides the tray onto the counter. Stepping back, he pulls his cap from his head, then retreats to the hall to remove his jacket. He transfers his smokes from his jacket to a pants pocket, and hums along to Peggy Lee.

Donna has moved the meatloaf into the dining-room. It sits in the middle of the table on a serving platter. As he takes his place at the table, she exits the kitchen with a bowl of vegetables in each hand. She puts them down, puts her hands in her underarms to pull off the oven mitts, then places them, and the apron she deftly removes, on the credenza behind her.

You should see what they're doing at the base, he tells Donna as he cuts the meatloaf and transfers slices to his plate. It's amazing, he says, We got this sled powered by rockets. I volunteered for the project and today I got to ride the sled. Two hundred miles per hour!

He spoons mash and peas onto his plate, and then drowns everything in gravy.

Two hundred miles per hour! he repeats; And then bang! A dead-stop in five feet. They said afterwards I hit about 18 G.

Is that dangerous? asks Donna.

He ignores her worried look, just as he did when he went off to Europe to fight the Nazis. It's important stuff, he tells her; We're making it safe for pilots to eject from jet fighters.

He stabs the air before him with his knife, and continues: it's all about going higher and faster, that's the kind of thing they're doing at the base. Pretty soon, they'll be going so high they'll be in outer space. We'll put a man up there in a few years, you bet. The Soviets will beat us to it, but that don't matter[1].

Yes, dear, says Donna.

☆

The Aerojet bottles light and the sled rolls forward, faster and faster and faster. The sergeant braces himself as acceleration presses him back into his seat. He stares ahead at the windshield, ignoring the landscape rushing past to either side. He's going faster than 200 miles an hour now. He cannot move a muscle.

Then the brakes engage.

He goes from 220 miles per hour to a stop in less than thirty feet. He can feel his eyeballs pull forward, his face strain to rip free of his skull. He suffers a red out. Later, they tell him he hit 20 G while braking. The harness holds— unlike on one of the dummy runs, when the harness snapped and sent Oscar Eightball 700 feet across the desert. Stapp has survived higher G, of course. For all the man's jokes and aphorisms, he won't allow anyone to try something he's not done himself. The sergeant admires the

---

[1] The first man in space was Soviet cosmonaut Yuri Gagarin, who launched from Baikonur Cosmodrome on 12 April 1961. Gagarin was a jet fighter pilot in the Soviet air force, as indeed were all the cosmonauts originally selected for the USSR's space programme. Though the Space Race was presented as non-military both by the USA and the USSR, the astronauts and cosmonauts were all military officers and the launch vehicles had been developed from ballistic missiles, rockets created for the sole purpose of destroying a distant enemy. Gagarin died in a MiG-15 crash in 1968, while training for his second flight in space. The cause of the crash remains a mystery, though the most likely reason appears to have been a close approach at supersonic speed by a fighter from a nearby air base. The Soviet air force has repeatedly denied this, perhaps too embarrassed to admit to causing the death of a beloved Hero of the Soviet Union. The first American in space was Alan B Shepard, a US Navy aviator, who flew a fifteen-minute sub-orbital hop on 5 May 1961.

major: he's tireless, indefatigable, boundlessly optimistic, and generous with his time, wisdom and medical skills. He's also a hard taskmaster.

The sun is shining, says Major Stapp, that means there's work to be done.

And so the sergeant was strapped onto the Gee Whiz, the rocket bottles lit, and he hurtled down the track at 220 mph. And came to a dead stop in fractions of a second.

He's woozy when they help him down from the rocket sled. His vision is still a little blurry, and he feels a headache building. He follows the others back to the control bunker, and stands and watches as the team pass around graphs from the plotter, and he knows those few seconds of speed, those tenths of a second of deceleration, they're drawn there on the paper and they make sense to the guys. He feels like a guinea pig, he *is* a guinea pig; he can't contribute knowledgeably to this conversation. But he knows there is a purpose to all this, a *good* purpose, one that will make things better for the pilots in their jet fighters.

At the end of the day, he drives his Mercury Eight through the whispering desert, following the shimmering blacktop from the air field to Lancaster through a world pregnant with possibility. He pulls up on his driveway, jumps out of the car and bounds through the front door into the house. Vaughn Monroe is singing about ghost riders in the sky on the radio.

Donna is in the kitchen. She has a pot roast on the counter. She turns as he enters. He crosses to her and she proffers a cheek to be kissed.

Smells great, he says, after giving her a peck.

It should do, she replies; it's been in the oven most of the afternoon.

Pretty soon, in about twenty years, he says, every kitchen will have a little oven on the counter that cooks food in a couple of minutes[2]. He snaps his fingers in illustration.

Don't be silly, she tells him, and turns back to her pot roast.

It's not silly, he insists; it'll cook the food right through in seconds. Then you'll have more time to do other things.

He heads into the dining-room and he thinks: progress is just so damn neat.

This is the sergeant's third run on the Gee Whiz. He can't say he's getting used to it, but it no longers frightens him so much. The fierce deceleration will be painful, but it will not cause any lasting harm. It will, however, save lives. He likes that his contribution to progress is so direct. He is risking his life—or, at least, risking injury—in order to safeguard others' lives. It makes him feel like a pioneer, like Wiley Post or Captain Yeager. He never made the cut for pilot, so this work he is doing now will not benefit him personally. Sometimes he dreams about flying one of the new jet fighters, like the F2H Banshee or the F-86 Sabre, and then he thinks about it flaming out and having to eject at 40,000 feet—and *that* must be a lot like these deceleration tests.

---

[2] The use of microwave radiation to heat food was accidentally discovered in 1945, when Percy Spencer, an engineer working on a military microwave radar transmitter, noticed that the chocolate bar in his pocket had melted. Radar had been developed prior to World War II in secret research programmes in the USA, Great Britain, Italy, Japan, France, the Netherlands, Germany and the Soviet Union, purely for its military application. The first microwave ovens were made commercially available in 1947, but they were nearly six feet tall, weighed 750 lb and cost the equivalent of $50,000 in today's money. The first home microwave oven did not appear until 1955 but it did not sell well, and it was not until 1967 that the first popular home model appeared. It cost $3,450 in today's dollars. In 1971, only 1% of homes possessed a microwave. By 1986, this figure was up to 25%. It is estimated that over 90% of homes now own one.

After the run, his ribs pain him and he thinks they might be cracked, so Major Stapp gives him a quick medical check-up and pronounces him fit. He aches all over, and there are lines of bruises across his torso, but everything is in working order. Sometimes, he feels a little dizzy for a second or two, but he only has to hold still a moment and it goes away. He is good at staying still. He fought for his country, kneeling for hours over twin Browning M2 .50 machine-guns at the end of a B-17 fuselage, cold, aching, legs cramping, eyes tearing up from staring at limitless sky, and knowing he must be vigilant to spot enemy fighters approaching from the rear. The Brits called him a "Tail End Charlie", but his commander knew he was the most important man on the ship.

Now he's the only man on this sled.

His speed renders the world unparseable, no meaning to be found in the rush of landscape and scrub and sand, even the distant mountains, dancing in the haze, fade in and out like glimpses of another reality. The concrete in which the rails sit shimmers in the heat like a river of blurred grey water. He cannot ahead because of the windsheield, but he pictures the rails arrowing to a point, unchanging despite the fact he is travelling at more than 200 miles per hour.

The clamps bite into the teeth as the sled hits the forty-five-foot braking section. The vehicle slams to a halt. He feels a slice of pain across his chest from the harness, his head jerks forward, his vision fills with scarlet. And that transcendental lightness as the G-forces lift, it feels like an out-of-body experience, as though he were drifting up to heaven on wings of sacrifice. But then the real world rudely inserts itself, pain anchoring him within his body, the bruises, the aches and twinges, and he waits patiently for the technicians to arrive to unbuckle him and pluck the wires from their recording instruments.

He follows them back to the control bunker, shrugging off any discomfort, assuring everyone he's fine and untroubled. The major is fiercely honest about the effects of high Gs—it's why he insists on running new test profiles himself before any volunteer gets a go—but to the sergeant: to have fought in Europe, and come home unscathed... It seems unpatriotic to complain about a few aches and pains and the odd bit of blurriness in his vision. This is, after all, the future they're building here. It's the lives of future jet fighter pilots they'll be saving. There's good in this. So he puts a brave smile on his face and emulates Major Stapp.

At the end of the day, he says goodbye to the guys, clambers into his Mercury Eight and roars out of the parking lot. Sailing through the desert, powered by a flathead V8, elbow out the window polished by the hot wind, he follows the blacktop through desolation to an oasis of progress—its grid of streets, its subdivisions of low-slung bungalows, its creature comforts in the midst of this harsh landscape. They have tamed the desert and they are taming the future. The sergeant is a part of it. He safeguarded the present for twenty-five missions with his twin Browning M2s; now he's part of the team corralling the world to come and the potential dangers within it.

He arrives home, turns off the engine, jumps from the car and strides into the house.

Donna is in the kitchen, holdinog a frying pan in which sizzles a large slab of steak. Frankie Laine is singing about the end of the road on the radio.

The sergeant kisses his wife, and ducks away laughing as she brandishes her carving fork at him.

I hit 22 G today, he tells her; I reckon I'm going to need all that steak.

She tuts, and prods the meat with her fork.

In fact, he adds, I reckon I could eat a whole horse today. I went so fast I built up a real appetite.

How much longer are you going to be on this project? she asks. She's not looking at him, but he hears the concern in her voice and, for one brief moment, he considers sharing everything with her... And then he looks her up and down, from her high-heeled pumps and stockinged calves to her blond Joan Crawford hairstyle, and he remembers he's there to protect her and keep her safe—from Nazis, from Reds, from whatever the world to come may throw at the two of them.

He shrugs and says, Does it matter? It's not dangerous.

Donna turns and jabs the carving fork in his direction. Not dangerous? she says. And I suppose the moon is made of green cheese too!

But she's smiling.

Of course, the Moon isn't made of green cheese, he tells her. When we put a man on the Moon[3]—more than one, in fact—he'll bring some moon rocks back and they'll be able to prove it.

Donna laughs. Don't be silly, she says. Put a man on the Moon? Wherever do you get these ideas from?

It is the sergeant's last day on Project MX981. With the increasing number of new jet aircraft being brought over to Muroc from Wright-Patterson AFB for test flying, he is needed back in the hangars. No more trips out here to the desert north of the base. No more riding the Gee Whiz and then feeling his entire body squeezed and crushed as the

---

[3] On 20 July 1969, two American astronauts landed on the Moon, the first human beings to ever do so. Although the first man to set foot on the lunar surface, Neil Armstrong, was a civilian, he had flown for the US Navy during the Korean War, flying 78 missions. In 1955, he became a test pilot for NACA at Edwards Air Force Base, flying research aircraft such as the X-1B and X-15, programmes funded in part by the US military with the intent of military applications. In 1958, Armstrong was selected for the US Air Force's Man In Space Soonest programme, and in 1962 was picked as a pilot for the Air Force's X-20 programme, although the craft was never built. Later that year, he was invited to join NASA's Astronaut Corps, and became the first civilian to do so. Armstrong's Lunar Module Pilot was Edwin 'Buzz' Aldrin, a colonel in the US Air Force. The third member of the crew, Lieutenant Colonel Michael Collins, USAF, remained in the command module in orbit about the Moon.

rocket sled slams to an abrupt halt.

He finds Major Stapp beside the track, overseeing technicians as they fit four Aerojet bottles to the rack at the rear of the sled. The sergeant does not disturb the man, but stands back and watches. He looks up the track, the two standard gauge rails narrowing to a point in the distance. And he remembers the journeys he has taken along that track, zooming toward where the rails appear to meet, knowing he will be brought to a sudden and violent stop before he can reach it. He imagines a world where those two rails do indeed join, where it is not just an optical illusion, a mirage. And he thinks about what that might do to the rocket sled and the person riding it.

It occurs to him time too is a track, and the future that illusionary point where the rails meet. Always visible, always ahead; never to be reached. The Gee Whiz fooled him into thinking he would get there... only to stop him dead just before he made it.

The rocket bottles have been fitted, and so the sergeant approaches Major Stapp and thanks him for allowing him to contribute. They shake hands, and Stapp makes a quip that prompts a smile. The sergeant steps back and throws a respectful salute. Stapp tells him if he ever needs help to drop by his office—there's no telling the long-term effects of all those Gs.

The sergeant nods and says, I'll do that, sir.

He turns about and walks back to his car. Behind him, he hears Stapp discussing the upcoming rocket sled run. They've come up with a new profile, so of course the major will insist on being the first to test it. The bravest man I ever met, the sergeant heard one pilot say of Stapp; and he feels the same way too. A dedicated man: a doctor, a scientist. It has been a pleasure, an education, working under him.

The sergeant reaches his car and turns back to look at the rocket sled on its track. Beyond it, the high desert stretches to the distant Sierra Nevadas, a flat tan landscape peppered with green scrub and hazed by the heat of the summer sun. He pulls down the bill of his cap, then taps out a cigarette from the pack in his breast pocket and pushes it between his lips. This desert is an unexpected place to build the future, but it's here they broke the Sound Barrier only eighteen months ago. And they'll do more. The sergeant feels certain of the good the rest of the century will bring. He holds that certainty close, it gives shape to his life—just as the Gee Whiz gave direction to it over three short rocket-powered journeys.

The Gee Whiz will continue its tests, carrying Major Stapp and other volunteers at high speed... and then bringing them to abrupt halts.

The sergeant wonders how those journeys will change the world[4].

---

[4] John Paul Stapp was dubbed "the fastest man on earth" when he reached a speed of 632 mph on the rocket sled at Holloman Air Force Base in 1954. He experienced 46.2 G when the sled braked. Both records stand to this day. Stapp proved that pilots could withstand up to 45 G of deceleration, and all cockpits, ejection seats and harnesses were subsequently redesigned to those higher tolerances. Stapp was also a principal advocate of safety belts in cars, and over the years gave 225 speeches on their benefits around the US. When mandatory seat-belts were signed into law in 1966 by President Lyndon B Johnson, Stapp was present at the signing. As indication, in 1940 there were twenty-five million licensed drivers in the US and 40,000 traffic deaths; by 2000 there were seventy-two million drivers and 42,000 deaths. When asked why he had ridden the rocket sled, Stapp said, "I have the missionary spirit. When asked to do something, I do it. I took my risks for information that will always be of benefit. Risks like that are worthwhile." He will also be remembered for coining Murphy's Law: "whatever can go wrong, will go wrong." He died peacefully at the age of 89 in 1999.

FAR VOYAGER

Every day for two hours, he positions himself before the observation window and gazes out, though there is nothing to see—only an unrelieved blackness across which are scattered the still silent beacons of distant stars. They slide past his view, travelling from left to right as the spacecraft rotates once every sixty minutes, keeping an even temperature across its skin. Not that "rotisserie mode" is necessary: the Sun is little more than a burning white dot a fraction of an inch across. This is all he has seen since *Voyager* left Saturn and its moons twenty-five years ago; it is his universe, and it is a bleak and unchanging and inhospitable place.

He always knows what to expect when he looks through the window, but deep in his heart, embarrassingly, shamefully, lurks some tiny kernel of hope he might one day see another spacecraft. An interstellar one perhaps; alien. But he knows it is silly, that even if humanity is not alone in the cosmos, the distances are too vast to cross, the intervening space too inimical, too impersonal. Yet it would be another first for him: First Contact, First Man to Meet an Alien. Or perhaps not. Given the advances on Earth since his launch in 1977, the MCC would likely know of any visitor to the Solar system long before he did. After all, his spacecraft is basic: it was engineered for reliability, not sophistication. And it has continued to function against all expectations for thirty-seven years; as, indeed, has he himself. Both have lasted much longer than even their most fervent champions in NASA had hoped.

Soon *Voyager* will reach the heliopause and he will become the first human being to travel into interstellar space. He has already journeyed the greatest distance of any person, has reached the farthest point from Earth of any person. He is the loneliest man in history, and has been for nearly four decades, and sometimes he asks himself why he fought to be sent on this mission...

And then, gazing at the stars as they smear across the observation window, the wonder of his situation steals upon him and he knows he would not wish to be anywhere else. He is floating in a tin can more than ten billion miles from Earth and moving further away with every passing second—

How could he not want to be here?

☆

After his daily vigil, he starts on the chores required to keep his home running. His day is driven by routine, without it he could not have survived this long. He pushes himself towards the hatch in the ceiling of the crew quarters, flies through the airlock module, and into the CM. Pulling himself down and strapping himself into the middle of the three seats before the instrument panel, he reaches for the checklist velcro'd above his head, then consults the Omega strapped about his wrist. The watch has kept time faithfully for four decades, though he has had to shorten the wrist-strap several times over the years. Like *Voyager* itself, it has continued to function for years on the edge of its operating envelope. It is a product of another time, he himself is a product of another time; and so too is this cramped conical chamber in which he sits, with its row of three canvas seats, its eleven-foot-wide instrumental panel in battleship grey, covered in dials and switches and barberpoles indicator lights. It is almost time for the Mission Control Center to call in—he keeps to Houston time aboard *Voyager*, has always kept to it, though a decade ago they handed off the project to JPL in California and he sometimes gets confused over the time-difference.

The radio squawks, and through the hiss of static he hears a scratchy voice. Hey there, Admiral, this is Ricardo Mendez at JPL calling in to see how things are up there, you know?

These engineers they have on capcom now have no concept of protocol. Sometimes they behave as if these are friendly telephone chats and not daily mission briefings. He doesn't like this habit of informality, he thinks it demeans his achievement, demeans all the work put in by the guys at NASA to put him here, days away from the heliopause, days away from leaving the Solar system.

Mendez—deaf of course to anything he might say—has carried on: According to my apps, your telemetry is all in the green, so I guess everything's still holding up after all these years. They sure built to last in those days, didn't they. Right, I've said all I'm going to say so I'll just wait for your reply, Admiral.

He assumes the engineers are young—it's difficult to tell given the poor quality of the audio—but the expressions they use, some of them are unfamiliar, the cultural references they drop most are indecipherable to him. They talk of movies and television shows and singers, and he's not heard of one of them; and so he sits there and listens and mourns the lost culture of his years on Earth. He thinks that only he remembers the movies and television shows and singers of his younger years and, to him, it is not nostalgia because he never moved forward, time never moved on for him. He is stuck in a cultural bubble not of his own making, but which is populated only by his memories.

They mention the web and blogs and cells and apps, and this is apparently the stuff of modern life; and it means zip to him. He cannot even imagine what it might possibly mean, how life back on Earth has changed so much these strange things have become ordinary, are now moulding the way people live. He imagines a prosperous world at peace, and clean cities and clean living and machines that do all the work, that bring people together, that make the world a smaller and more manageable and friendlier place, in which strangeness is no cause for fear but food for curiosity. And then he tries to tally that with a space programme that, but for himself, has never left Low Earth Orbit, in which the nations of the Earth send people into space but none has ever revisited the Moon.

He remembers one capcom years before who said, Ah hell damn it, my mouse has stopped working, let me get someone from desktop support. He had to wait over twelve hours wondering if he was going mad, if cosmic rays had finally scrambled his neurons, and he was now hearing something other than what was being said. Or perhaps it was the capcom whose hold on sanity had fractured at that precise moment, perhaps triggered by the realisation he was talking to a person billions of miles away, way past the orbit of Pluto.

But *this* he does understand: a printed checklist, spiral-bound. He doesn't need it, of course: he has performed this routine almost every day for forty years, it is hard-wired in. It's like he has his own read-only rope-memory somewhere in his head, and all those twists and turns of copper wire means he knows exactly what every switch, keypad and controller on the Apollo Command Module's instrument panel means and what it operates. He has spent so many years poring over the circuit diagrams for the CM's various sub-systems he suspects he could draw many of them from memory. He knows everything there is to know about his home: he is the world's greatest expert on *Voyager*, he is intimate with its every characteristic planned and unintended—not to mention all those that are a consequence of its age and the long journey it has undertaken.

Finishing the checklist, he re-attaches it to the velcro above him. He now has a fifteen-hour wait before his words reach California, and are heard by Mendez, and a further fifteen hours before the capcom's reply reaches him. He is used to this form of communication now; it's no different to sending letters abroad, or messages on cassette tape through the mail. The thought prompts regret: the cassette tapes he brought with him have long since perished, and he has not heard music for decades, has only the chorus of pings and pops and creaks of *Voyager* as she sails through interplanetary space to fill the silence of the stars. During the early years of his journey, music would fill the empty hours, the empty space within, and the joy of the songs, despite the muddy sound from the little cassette player's speaker, would give him something to fix upon, something to fill the days that never ended. No longer.

He has learned to live without it; he feels more at one with the vacuum outside by sharing its absence of sound. Sometimes the thought makes him angry, and he weeps bitter tears as he gazes out of the observation window and reflects on the irrelevance of mankind in the universe's scheme of things, while his face is reflected in the glass, ethereal and ghostly, ironic commentary on the fragility of his world.

Other time, the silence amuses him and he knows he will last another day, he will be the first man to leave the Solar system, he will be the first person from Earth to travel into interstellar space.

☆

For thirty-seven years and one month, *Voyager* has sped outwards from Earth. The spacecraft picked up additional speed from a gravity assist from Saturn in August 1980, and now travels towards interstellar space at 10.5 miles per second, around 38,185 mph. Within *Voyager*, such frantic velocity is not apparent, as there is nothing against which to judge the spacecraft's speed. When he stares out of the observation window, the only movement he sees is that caused by *Voyager*'s rotation, and several times he has buckled himself into the rotating chair before the window and spent hours looking for any change in any of the objects within view.

But they are too far away, too small, too insignificant.

He remains seated in the rotating chair now and, looking up, he sees the hatch in the ceiling and knows that beyond it, beyond the upturned Apollo spacecraft docked there, lies the heliopause, the boundary where the solar wind is stopped by the interstellar medium, the true limit of the Sun's planetary system. Beneath the latticed floor to which the chair is secured is another deck, and below that the Phoebus reactor and nuclear rocket engine. The deck below was once filled with stores, but he has consumed the bulk of them during the past four decades, though the tank of recycled water remains mostly full. It is shaped like a doughnut so he can hunker in its centre during flares, safe from the deadly particles sleeting through space. He has perhaps another four or five years left of food; the Closed Ecological Life Support System, however, will keep him in water and air for decades yet.

He is approaching his ninety-first birthday, and he had not expected to live this long, no one had expected him to live this long. A life in zero gravity has extended his life, and fortunately he has not developed cancer from the cosmic radiation. His fitness has gone, however: his legs are withered and near useless, his chest capacity has shrunk, his arms are like those of a skeleton corded with wire, and his skin dry and liver-spotted like old leather.

He lifts a hand and gazes at it, and remembers when it was strong, when it gripped the control column of a T-38 with casual confidence. He does not miss flying—he is flying all the time now, and without an aircraft too. Admittedly he misses the speed, the power, and he has forgotten how to walk: what it felt like, putting one foot before the other, the flexing of muscles, the fight against gravity. Most of all he misses golf. He misses the swing of the arms, the twist of the torso, the whip of the wrist, and the thwack as the club hits the ball. He misses the satisfaction of seeing the ball travel far and where he aimed it, straight down the middle, towards the pin. For him, it epitomises the *physicality* of his past life, his physical prowess: running, lifting, throwing, making snap decisions.

He misses the competition.

And then he realises he is a winner, the biggest winner of all. He has taken the great prize: to be the first man to leave the Solar system. He knows the US space programme foundered after Space Station Freedom was built—the capcoms told him so: foreign wars and budget deficits and lack of public interest. It seems likely the next person to leave the Solar system will not do so for many centuries, so his first will stand for hundreds of years, perhaps even longer.

Oh wow, hey sorry, I forgot it was my turn as capcom. Sorry about all the noise. I'm out with some friends, in a bar. Let me find somewhere a bit quieter. How's that? Can you hear me now? Hey, I'm sorry but it completely slipped my mind, you know, that this thing precesses, like every time you call it's a different time of day. It's like eight in the evening here, so I'm calling from my cell. Don't worry, I got all the apps on it I need to monitor your telemetry and—let me just have a quick check—yeah, sure, everything's in the green, looking good. It's been real interesting this, you know, talking to you every day, I mean you launched before I was born, but I looked *Voyager* up online and it's kind of cool you know? And the science is real fascinating, but my internship finishes soon, and I guess they'll hand you over to some new guy. So thanks and good luck, and it's been a real pleasure working with you. I guess I don't envy you—I mean I could never do what you did, but it's kind like touching history and that's cool, that's going to stay with me for like ever.

☆

Today, he changed one of the molecular sieves which scrub the carbon dioxide from the air. They are prone to clogging; he can only clean them so many times before they must be replaced. The system which recycles water is much more durable, although over the decades his water consumption has dropped, and he suspects his kidneys could no longer cope with the intake of water normally required by a person of his size and weight.

Afterwards, he prepares and eats a meal—he no longer bothers checking the labels as he can no longer taste the contents of the packets. Then he returns to the CM, settles in the middle seat and thinks about his daily log entry. In his mind, he considers the words he would write down had he any paper to write upon. Somewhere in one of the lockers beneath him are two decades' worth of logbooks. He made a daily entry because it was SOP, but he never really understood for whose benefit he did so, as a return to Earth was never part of the mission profile. Perhaps in some distant future, when mankind has finally made it to the stars, a spacecraft will stumble across a cold dark *Voyager* tumbling through the void.

He will not have another first stolen from him; it is what has kept him alive for so long—yes he was the first man to visit the Jupiter and Saturn systems, but that was not enough. He never forgave the goddamned Soviets for beating him into space. He had pushed so hard for that first flight, even though it was just a short suborbital hop, fifteen minutes up and down; and then the pencil-necks had put back the launch. They all said he was the first American into space, and that was important—Kennedy even gave him a medal for it—but he knew he was only the *second* man in space. He could not sleep for days afterwards, enraged at his failure to be there first.

And then the final indignity: Ménière's Disease, grounded. He refused to give up the dream, though his condition had stolen it from his grasp; he would not walk away. They offered him a position in the Astronaut's Office, and he took it because it kept him close, it kept him in the running, it kept him in the loop. They called him the "icy commander" but if only they'd known the control it took to be civil, to maintain the punishingly high standards to which he held himself. The surgery should have cured it— had it done so, he would have fought for a shot at the Moon. He didn't care whose toes he trod on: one of those Apollo missions would have been his, no one could have refused him. But that quack in California fixed nothing and it wasn't until a couple of years, a couple of doctors, after the first attempt, that he'd finally been given a clean bill of health.

By then there were no Apollo missions left to fly.

They said he was ubiquitous during those years—at every meeting, every briefing, speaking to everyone. He would not be denied. He was oldest member of the astronaut corps, yes, would be over fifty on the planned launch date; but he had plenty of years left in him, more than enough to reach Jupiter and Saturn.

The Voyager mission had been a surprise

announcement, the last gasp of the Apollo era, the desperate grab by NASA for the funds remaining in the bottom of the barrel. Two Saturn S-IVB stages were converted—one into Skylab, and the other into *Voyager*'s crew quarters. He'd missed Gemini, Apollo and Skylab, he would not miss this. He gave them no choice. This would be a one-way mission, and he was the ideal candidate—he knew it, he made sure everyone knew it.

Sometimes, he wonders what else he might have missed. The Earth has changed since he left, changed in ways unknown to him, and the mutating vocabularies of the capcoms has led to increasingly surreal conversations. He was never an imaginative man—NASA did not want imaginative men in its astronaut corps—but it is the only escape he has, and decades of use have honed his use of it to a fine edge. He tries to imagine what the cities of Earth now look like. Modern and functional, he thinks, with clean lines, sharp and square or curved and swooping, polished grey concrete, blue and green glass, white surfaces which shine in the sun, plazas ringed by the featureless faces of tall buildings, greenswards which lead the eye to gleaming domes. He remembers photographs of Brasilia, scenes from the film *Rollerball*—great buildings of grey concrete as though they had been hewed direct from a city's substance, sleek monorails zipping everywhere on pylons above streets busy with pedestrians, automobiles that look like jet fighters, jet fighters that look like rocket planes, jet liners crossing the Atlantic in a couple of hours and jet bombers over Moscow just as quickly. Except the world is at peace now: no World War Three, no Cold War even.

He thinks of happy, prosperous people in happy, prosperous homes, though sometimes he suspects the future he has missed has not proven so bright. True, the capcoms to whom he talks all seem very self-assured and happy; but what are they not telling him? He never believed in World War Three, he never subscribed to Mutually Assured Destruction; Soviet technology had never in his estimation been up to the job, and the US Administration would never have the balls to strike first. He much prefers the future he has imagined. It consoles him as he drifts about *Voyager*'s silent interior.

Hey wow this is so cool, I'm talking to the spaceman. How far away are you? Billions of kilometres, right? Uh, of course, you can't answer. It says here it's going to take fifteen hours for this message to reach you. Man that's got to be a real bitch. It's a pity you don't have a webcam or anything then we'd be able to see each other, but I'm reading all about *Voyager* here and, wow, that's like archaic tech, it's totally amazing it's still working. I seen one of those old Apples once and they're just total junk, you got to wonder how people used them. Putting you on the internet was a really cool idea. They have this interactive animation of your flight, with popups and embedded videos and even transcripts of all your radio messages. Hey, is it okay if I do my school project on you? Can I ask you some questions for it?

He remembers the launches: two Saturn V rocket stacks, each 363 feet tall, each with 8,500,000 pounds of thrust, one to throw the crew quarters into orbit, another for the Apollo spacecraft and Phoebus nuclear rocket. He recalls lying on his back in the CM, gazing up through the polycarbonate of his helmet at the instrument panel. He no longer knows where his spacesuit is. In one of the lockers in the CM, he presumes; he has not used it since he passed the Asteroid Belt. He wanted to go EVA when he reached Jupiter, but the MCC nixed it because of the radiation hazard. Now he expects the spacesuit is unusable, the rubber bladder too fragile to hold air, the metal connectors rusted and corroded. It's been over thirty years and the spacesuits were not designed to last forever.

It is not the only piece of equipment he has outlasted.

Some days he wishes he had been on flight status during the Moon missions. He has witnessed more wonders than the twenty-seven men who left Earth orbit aboard Apollo, but he would have liked to have stood on the surface of the Moon. Those missions changed their lives, he remembers talking to them on the subject; but his life has not changed substantially in decades. Then he recalls what he has seen on his journey to the stars: Jupiter at 217,000 miles, volcano eruptions on Io, the ice chasms of Ganymede, the rings of Saturn, so many moons, moons beyond counting.

A few years ago, he was interviewed by some guy writing a book on the Space Race. He had been surprised people were still interested in it. He remembers the apathy after Apollo 17, the way the national will Kennedy had created evaporated after Apollo 11. He knows from the capcoms he is no international hero but a forgotten relic of a bygone age. He answered the writer's questions—it was not an interview, but a sequence of monologues. Just like email, the writer tells him, though what that means who knows. Then the writer says, Those photos you took of the moons of Saturn: it must have been really cool to see them like that, especially the one that looks like the Deathstar.

Deathstar? He had to ask for an explanation, and when he heard it he was once again reminded of all he had missed. It was a reference to a movie which had been released several months before he launched. He vaguely remembers hearing about it: another dumb sci-fi flick, of no interest to him. To have proven so popular it is remembered decades later is a shock.

The cast of kids' movies are popular heroes and remain so for forty years. Mankind's only real live interstellar explorer has been consigned to the trash can of history.

☆

He sits before the window for his daily observations but today he will not move. The MCC has told him, and his instruments confirm their findings, that today he will pass through the heliopause and into the bow shock. No one knows what to expect, no one knows what he will find on the other side, no one knows if *Voyager* will even survive the transition.

He straps himself into the chair, and locks it so it faces towards the window, while the stars drift placidly across the glass as the spacecraft rotates. When he left Earth the existence of the heliopause was unknown, even now it is mostly theoretical. *Voyager* is the first spacecraft to have come so far and her scientific instruments are crude and not especially discriminatory.

The S-IVB which forms the crew quarters begins to creak. Flashes of light streak across his vision even with his eyes closed. He can taste copper and iron in the back of his throat, and feel a weakness in his guts. From the hatch into the CM, he hears a clacking as the barber-poles trip. Every light on every piece of equipment in the crew quarters turns red.

A curtain of light, a bright aurora, shimmers across the observation window, and he sees blues and greens and yellows and oranges and red. It sparkles and scintillates and he thinks, this is it, this is the bow shock. Soon he will be in interstellar space, no longer protected by the solar wind.

The veil of brightness coruscates like fire and then fades away to the black of space. A city, he sees a city spread across the heavens. It is silvery-grey and made of cubes and cuboids and trapezoids, made of concrete polished until it shines with a nacreous light. Green glass glows like the heart of a forest, blue glass ripples like the sea off an Hawaiian beach. Great sterile white domes and the swooping organic curves of towers and monuments. Monorail tracks stitched neatly across the spaces between buildings. He looks out on this city and he knows his mission has come to an end, he has reached the limits of the Solar system, the limits of his existence.

He is the first man of Earth to enter interstellar space. And now he no longer feels alone.

RED DESERT

The MRV bounces across rusty sand, rattling every part of its aluminium chassis, but the only sound Anna Louise Givens hears is the whisper of the fan in her spacesuit's backpack. According to the Mars Roving Vehicle's control panel, they're travelling at fifteen kilometres per hour, heading due north, and the batteries are running at 140 Amp-hours. A plume of red sprays up from the rear wheels as Wesley pushes the T-bar to the right. The front of the vehicle hits a low sandy ridge, pitches up and breaks through its crusted peak. Wesley and Anna Louise do not speak, there is no need. They are secure in each other's presence, even enclosed in spacesuits, so wrapped in layers of rubber, Mylar and Beta Cloth they can neither touch each other nor the world about them.

Wesley abruptly breaks into song: I was driving on Mars one day, in the merry merry month of May—

It's February, rebukes Anna Louise.

February doesn't rhyme, Wesley replies, with unassailable logic. And he laughs.

She feels his joy. Even now, a day after landing, Anna Louise finds it hard to believe she is on Mars. About her she sees pale red landscape, rocks and stones in russet, copper, burgundy and a dirty reddish-brown for which she has no name. She wants to run her fingers through the red sand, just to prove she is really here. The decade of training with her husband, Wesley Jefferson Givens, the six months on a transfer orbit across the inner Solar System... and then the anti-climactic descent in the MEM from Mars orbit.

When Anna Louise stepped out of the airlock and stood on the sinuous curves written on the Martian surface by the Mars Excursion Module's descent engine, it was so like the simulations it confused her and she fluffed her first line. It was only when her body finally accepted the lesser gravity that she knew for certain:

She was on Mars. She was the first person to step onto the Martian surface.

They broke protocol doing that. Mission Control complained, of course. As commander, Wesley was expected to take the first step onto the surface, but he gave his wife the honour. There was no silliness in the MEM over who would find it easier to exit given the way the hatch opened. NASA learnt that lesson with the Apollo Moon landings.

Though the MRV is based on Apollo's Lunar Roving Vehicle, this is not the Moon. There is colour here, albeit not much. The ground is a hard and flat desert, littered with rocks, with a thin crust across which wisps of sand skitter. The sky is a peculiar shade of washed-out rose, shading to black at the zenith. This landscape is as magnificent, as awe-inspiring, as the Colorado Plateau—but so empty and lifeless it seems to suck the vitality from Anna Louise. She grabs for the frame of her seat as the MRV hits a bump and jolts briefly into the air. Wesley apologises but does not pull back on the T-bar to lower their speed.

In this fashion, they bounce and career across the Martian desert toward Ganges Mensa, the low mesa they are scheduled to explore. They have already taken samples of the sand and rock surrounding the MEM, but now they must travel further afield. Anna Louise is reminded of training simulations, jouncing around Monument Valley in a Jeep Cherokee, pretending the light overalls and fibreglass helmets they wore were spacesuits. Perversely, the ride here is more comfortable—the ground is a little smoother, her spacesuit keeps her at a comfortable temperature, the light does not hurt her eyes, the lesser gravity means she sits lighter in her seat. She smiles at the memory of those days of sweat and toil, practicing to use the tools they must use here, collecting rocks and calling in spot identifications to "Mission Control", finding the narrative written in the landscape and trying to give it a voice...

Not that this spacesuit fits as well as it should, despite being specially tailored for her. She lost weight, as did Wesley, during the trip to Mars, during those endless days of zero gravity. The spacesuit's bladder is no longer as snug as it was back on Earth, and now rubs in places it didn't rub before.

Anna Louise is conscious of the restricted view given her by her helmet, of the curved expanse of polycarbonate centimetres from her face, of the hums and whirrs and gurgles and hisses in her backpack life-support system. Her hands already ache from the inflated gloves and she can feel the tips of her fingers beginning to numb from a combination of cold and the constant banging against the thimbles. She has already lost one fingernail, and will likely lose the rest before she gets back to Earth. It is a small price to pay.

Because Anna Louise is on Mars.

The MRV hits a bump. Wesley, she thinks, was a better driver than this back home. In fact, he was usually content

67

to let her drive most of the time. But she gave him this, control of the MRV on their first drive across the Martian sands, since she set was first to set foot on the surface.

Small red sand devils ghost across the landscape, springing up from nothing and returning to nothingness moments later. Yet the air seems so clear, distant objects boasting sharp edges, a gelid lucidity to the view before them. And then clarity is gone in an instant as dust flurries up into the air, blurring the landscape. The MRV powers through rills of dark brown, snakes as it hits patches of soft rust-coloured sand, and then jerks forward. Eventually, they reach the foot of the mensa and Wesley slews the vehicle to a halt. The chassis rocks as he clambers from his seat, and Anna Louise disembarks and turns to see Wesley walking away with that curious balletic waddle they've been forced to adopt in the pressurised spacesuits in the one-third gravity.

She leaves him to get on with his assigned tasks, she has her own work to do. So she heads off in the opposite direction, a long-handled scoop in one hand and a box for soil samples in the other. She watches the ground as she skips along, it is pristine, touched only by the wind and, perhaps at some point in its long history, a meteorite or piece of ejecta. No, not ejecta—there are no craters in this area, beside this mensa. She stops and then pulls back her foot, leaving a sharp boot-print in the red sand. She gazes down at the mark she has made and wonders how long it will remain. In a fit of perversity, she uses the scoop to take sample of sand from the heel of the boot-print, spoiling its lines. But there is a trail of boot-prints behind her, and wherever she goes she will leave yet more. There is nothing she can do about it—she and Wesley have despoiled Mars.

But, she tells herself, this is far too implacable, too harsh, a landscape for two humans to have much impact.

☆

Their landing site is just south of the equator, around 70° west, halfway between the lip of Ophir Chasma to the south, and Ganges Mensa to the north, on the southern edge of Lunae Planum. This is Mars' high desert, some 4,000 metres above datum, a flat plain scattered with rocks, lines of catenae and the occasional individual large crater. The big draw is Ophir Chasma, an offshoot of Candor Chasma, which is itself an offshoot of Valles Marineris. It is ten kilometres deep. In the second week of their mission timeline, Anna Louise and Wesley are scheduled to visit the chasma and study the layering of the rocks forming its walls. Scientists on Earth have already determined the region dates back to early Hesperian times, but they do not know if it was caused by volcanic or sedimentary processes.

Today, the mission protocol calls for a drive west, toward Juventae Dorsa, an open plain. They left the MRV recharging overnight, and they have plenty of juice in the batteries. This is what they will be doing for the next twenty-six days, driving around on the surface of Mars, to the limits of the MRV's range, exploring the geology of the areas they visit. It is only *where* they are doing this that is remarkable. On Mars. The Red Planet. Earth's neighbouring world, and 54.6 million kilometres from home at its nearest approach.

Anna Louise felt every one of those kilometres during the trip from Earth. Their flight-path was longer, of course—they were on an opposition-class mission, which meant they launched when Mars was on the other side of the Sun, and took 180 days to catch up to the Red Planet. Anna Louise and Wesley have been comfortable in each other's company for over a decade, their marriage is solid, they are *compatible*, their partnership a true synergy of give and take and compromise and empathy. And sex. And ambition. They are both one gestalt being and two separate people, they could not have survived the journey to Mars otherwise.

Anna Louise is driving the MRV today. She brings the

vehicle to a gentle halt on the dorsa, and they both climb from their seats. For the next hour or so, they wander about, their boots crunching through the caliche, kicking up the fine red sand.

Hey, says Wesley, I can see a crater, pretty good one, looks fresh.

Fresh? asks Anna Louise.

She turns about and sees he is standing at the top of a gentle rise in the ground, a low mound which stretches several hundred metres to either side of him.

A million years old, maybe, Wesley says. I'm going to have a look.

She watches him disappear over the brow of the hill, his white spacesuit, now liberally smeared with orange dust, stepping lower and lower as it rocks side to side, until even the rounded white crown of his helmet has dropped out of sight.

Don't go too far, she warns him.

It's only half a kilometre, he responds. Nothing to it.

Anna Louise turns back to her own prospecting. She hears a grunt from Wesley, loud enough to trigger the VOX, and wonders if he has perhaps stumbled or fallen. Another grunt, this one sounding frustrated, soon follows and she decides he is okay. The sound prompts a wan smile as she remembers last night, their first attempt at making love since landing on Mars. But they were both too tired, too sore, too unused to making love in gravity after six months of freefall—even in Mar's low gravity. Though Wesley swore at his failure, Anna Louise knew she would not have been able to respond, and found more comfort in his body pressed passively against hers than she would have done from intercourse.

She searches for unusual rocks in the sand—both are hoping to find the Martian equivalent of Apollo 15's "Genesis Rock", but Anna Louise, who consistently proved better at geology than Wesley during training, Anna Louise suspects there is little in the immediate area older than the early Amazonian, perhaps two billion years old. Remembering the trouble Wesley had reading the story written in the landscape back in Monument Valley, she says, Are you at that crater yet, Wesley?

There is no reply.

Wesley? Are you there?

Perhaps he did fall, perhaps he damaged his radio. She waits, expecting to see the dome of his helmet rise above the horizon, but the brow of the hill remains unbroken. He might not know his radio is broken, she thinks; he might be trying to talk to me now.

Wesley, I cannot hear you, she says. Please return to the MRV.

She gives him ten minutes but he does not reappear. She drops her scoop and moves forward, pushing off strongly with each foot, using her ankles as the spacesuit has little play in the knees. She bounces toward the MRV, and then past it, following Welsey's boot-prints in the sand, a clear line of them, already softening as the wind brushes across them. She cannot feel the breeze, the air here is too thin, two hundred times thinner than Earth's—at such low pressure, a hurricane would feel like a light breath of air.

She toils up the rise, her heartbeat elevated, and knows Houston will soon be demanding to know the reason for the change in her biometric data. But now she is at the lip of the hill, and below her is a flat slope of ochre sand and rocks, leading down to the raised rim of a crater, just as Wesley said, some five hundred metres away. She cannot see his boot-prints, the ground looks untrodden. She hurries forward, and within a step or two, she is trying to run, beginning to panic. She needs to find her husband, she needs to see Wesley, she has to know he is okay. She stumbles and pitches forward, hitting the dirt hard despite the low gravity. She lies there on her front, winded, and she frightens herself into a cold sweat as she realises how easily she might have cracked the polycarbonate of her helmet on a rock...

She struggles to her feet, and it takes several goes so she's sweating hard by the time she's upright. She remembers that grunt Wesley made over the radio, she's scared he might be lying face-down somewhere inside that crater. She carries on, this time more carefully, and on reaching the crater's rim grabs its lip with both hands and pulls herself up—

The crater is about eighty metres in diameter, its basin-shaped interior dropping to ten metres below her in the centre. The rim is less than two metres higher than the ground around and about the crater.

Frantically, she scans the crater. It is empty.

She gives it a second inspection, more diligently, alert for even the hint of white.

Nothing.

Ana Louise pushes herself away from the crater rim. She looks back along the route she took to reach the crater. The ground is flat, the pink rocks scattered about it too small to hide anything.

No Wesley.

The rapid thudding of her heartbeat seems to fill her helmet, and her backpack's fan whirs into a higher gear as her temperature rises. She must *think*, she tells herself, she must be *calm*. She takes several deep breaths, in through the nose, out through the mouth. She sips some water from the spout by her chin, to moisten a mouth suddenly turned painfully dry. She will do a circuit of the crater, she decides, it's only eighty metres across, that's... The mental arithmetic needed to calculate its circumference, $2\pi r$, about 250 metres, helps steady her.

Professional, cool and composed, she walks the crater's circumference; but she finds nothing, she finds no sign of Wesley, no clue to his fate. She climbs the hill to its summit, and looks down at the MRV, but no, he has not returned to it. She gazes at the uptilted dish of the high gain antenna on MRV. Everything she and Wesley have said—which, admittedly, has not been much—has been transmitted from their spacesuits to the MRV, then to the MEM and up to the comms sat they left in orbit about Mars, and thence to Earth.

Houston, she says, Houston, we have a problem.

☆

Houston insists and Anna Louise is keen to oblige, so she spends a further two hours searching the dorsa around and about the MRV and the crater, but there is no trace of Wesley. She can see to the distant horizon in all directions from the top of that low hill, the dorsa is flat, the highest crater rim no more than two metres high. Wesley's white spacesuit would be plainly visible, even with its streaks of Martian dirt. Reluctantly, she drives the MRV back to the MEM, her air is running short, she is exhausted, she aches everywhere, running in the spacesuit, falling in the spacesuit, has taken its toll. Her body feels numb, drained, but her mind is buzzing—and yet everything seems flat, unreal, like stage scenery. She knows this is no simulation—the gravity tells her so, and there's no way Houston could fake that umber sky, so dark at the zenith, with stars that shine like bright inquisitive eyes.

Once at the MEM, on the short ladder to the airlock door, looking up at the spacecraft's cone-shaped alien presence, like an Apollo Command Module writ large but painted white, now decorated with red lines and streaks from wind-carried sand... she baulks at entering, knowing it is empty within and will remain so even after she has passed through the door. But she has no choice. Inside, her spacesuit carefully stored in the airlock, she strips off her Liquid Cooling Garment, gives herself a sponge bath, and then dresses in a Constant Wear Garment and fabric slippers. She climbs the ladder to the ascent module cabin and settles in her seat before the instrument panel. Wesley is—*was*—the pilot/commander, though Anna Louise trained for just this eventuality: she can fly the MEM ascent module to orbit, if necessary.

She picks up the comms cap from the cabin-floor, pulls it on over her head, and plugs the cable into the instrument panel. It is time to make a full report. She switches the circuit to S-Band.

I don't know where he's gone, she says. And she marvels at her own calmness.

Houston, I searched the area thoroughly, she adds. Wesley, ah, Commander Givens, has gone, disappeared. Completely.

They will need more information, she tells herself. She is still not thinking clearly. She must maintain her icy calm, she must show she is made of the Right Stuff. Houston, she says... She recounts every step she took since leaving the MEM that morning, even though Houston have it all there in front of them, in manuals and mission protocols, as if she could do anything here on Mars that has not been planned and timed and scheduled to the minute. She tells them what they already know, in the hope that doing so will trigger a memory, provide a clue to Wesley's disappearance.

Now she has to wait eight minutes for a response from Mission Control.

They ask her all the obvious questions, and she answers them patiently. They are not here, they do not believe her, they think she is mistaken. Her biometric data proves she is as fit and well as she was the day before, but it cannot measure or record her mental state. She assures them, as placidly as she can, that she searched as well as she was able and found no trace of her husband.

Could something have taken him? Houston asks.

This world is dead, Anna Louise assures them. We've seen no evidence of native life or any other visitors beside ourselves.

Eventually, Mission Control brings the conversation—though to describe these calls and responses, each eight minutes apart, as a "conversation" is farcical—around to

74

the subject they have all been trying to avoid. Anna Louise cannot go home. Not just yet. The mission plan calls for thirty days on the Martian surface, and the MTV does not have enough fuel for anything other than the planned free return transfer orbit back to Earth. So she must stay here on Lunae Planum for another four weeks, and continue as if nothing were out of the ordinary.

As if the word "ordinary" applied...

Returning to the habitat toroid in the lower half of the MEM, she stands at one of the horizon windows, gazes out onto red sands and briefly imagines herself on some training exercise in the Arizona or Nevada desert. House and husband a short flight distant, a matter of hours in a T-38 or F-102. But Wesley is not there, nor is he here; Wesley has gone—

No, Wesley is *dead*. There is no other explanation. It is time to grieve for him. And, on cue, Anna Louise's vision begins to blur, as if rain is falling on Mars' arid red sands for the first time in millions of years. She is alone now, a widow, and the most solitary human being in the history of her race. She is more than a hundred million kilometres from home. She cries for herself as much as she cries for Wesley; and she is glad that Houston cannot hear her. She puts a hand up to the horizon window, and the outside chill transmits itself through the thick polycarbonate to her fingers. She welcomes the cold, it echoes the hollowness she feels inside. Turning about, she regards her surroundings, this banana-shaped tube wrapped around the ascent module's rocket engine, her home. It contains everything she needs for the next month; it will sustain her—the air she breathes, food, water... and a full schedule of activities.

The schedule, she acknowledges, more than anything else will likely save her.

☆

Anna Louise pulls open the airlock hatch, although she has yet to shed her spacesuit. She unlocks and lifts off her helmet, and exhales loudly. As if conjured by her entrance, Wesley is sitting at the fold-out desk by the galley. He looks round as, standing in the hatchway, she begins to unhook the connectors on the front of her spacesuit.

A good day? he asks.

You should see the chasma, she tells him. It's magnificent. So... so... *enormous.*

Her language has failed her, even though she is still abrim with the landscape she has spent the day exploring. Ophir Chasma—ten thousand metres deep at its deepest! Three hundred and eighty kilometres long! Sheer cliffs thousands of metres high, footed with slopes of scree that stretch for tens of kilometres! It is the Grand Canyon writ large, writ *huge.* Standing beside the chasma, such an unimaginably enormous bite taken from the landscape, she felt dizzy simply gazing at it. Her heart seemed to swell, as if trying to digest the sheer scale, to beat faster and faster, so much so Houston ten minutes later asked her what had happened...

But now she is back in the MEM, it is the end of the day, and once she has this spacesuit stowed away, has given herself a sponge bath and dressed, then she will climb up to the ascent module cabin and give her daily report to Houston. With each passing day, she has begun adding texture and narrative to her EVA reports, her impressions, her feelings, her responses to this landscape she has come to love with a deep, and entirely selfish, possessiveness—though still it scares her with its size, its grandeur, its lifelessness. She slouches in her seat in the ascent module, and monologues her way through her day, and it feels like she is telling Wesley, though she knows he is downstairs pottering about, doing something at the desk, his presence making the hab module more homely and her return to it at the end of each EVA more bearable.

After her report to Houston and some banter

punctuated by eight minutes of silence, she clambers back down the ladder to the hab module. Her heart lifts as she spots Wesley, still at the desk, and she stands in the doorway and watches him, the comforting spread of his shoulders, the steady competence implicit in his straight-backed posture, his short-cut hair, his firm jaw with its pale dusting of stubble, the guileless blue of his eyes. She crosses to him, hooks her arms about his neck, and bends to peck him on his crown. Her aches and pains are forgotten, her black-and-blue hands, the fingertips bloody like a torture victim's, no longer send their constant messages of pain.

Her mind has room only for Mars and for Wesley.

Dinner is, as usual, another tray pulled from a locker and shoved into a microwave. Wesley watches her eat, so she pretends to enjoy the meal though she cannot really taste it and the texture tells her nothing of what it is. Anna Louise doesn't know how she would have coped without her husband's presence. She's been on Mars now for two weeks, nearly half of her planned surface time. She's millions of kilometres from Earth, with no hope of rescue; she could not have done this on her own. Though she has never been especially gregarious, neither is she is the type to make a good hermit—absolute solitude would, she thinks, be debilitating. Until coming to Mars, it had not occurred to her quite how lonely it was possible to be.

She reaches out and squeezes Wesley's shoulder. She's glad he's around, he sustains her.

So the Martian days pass, each moment plotted and timed and scheduled, and though the mission protocol has changed, though Anna Louise must now take risks previously considered untenable, the EVAs continue, the exploration of Mars goes on. Anna Louise takes out the MRV and collects rocks, performs experiments, records the daily results from the MSEP. And after each EVA, she returns to the MEM, and Wesley is there to add an air of easy domesticity to the cramped interior of the spacecraft. She gets into the habit of going over the day with him as she eats, before making her report to Houston, and it helps her to order her thoughts, to shape her recollection of her activities, so that she can give narrative coherence to each moment she spends on Mars' surface. After each report, Houston asks how she is coping, will she be able to keep to the schedule, get everything done according to the mission protocol. She assures them she is fine, Wesley is helping... and they profess not to understand.

Sometimes, based on her reports, Mission Control makes changes to her daily protocol; sometimes, based on her biometric data, they restructure her activities. Of late, they've been scheduling her more time exercising, as if tramping around the Martian landscape in a spacesuit, even in one third of a G, isn't exertion enough. But she's happy to obey the voices from Earth. She thinks of herself now as a recording angel, here on Mars to document it, to *witness* it, for her people, her world, her race. She is a piece of equipment, built by a NASA contractor, programmed by Houston, fuelled by Wesley's presence.

Without the mission protocol, she would not have survived; without Wesley, she would not have survived. He keeps her grounded, motivates her to continue each day until the last day when the MEM will launch from the surface, will rendezvous with the MTV in orbit, will fire a Trans Earth Injection burn, and then the free return trajectory home.

Another day and she climbs into her spacesuit, not an easy task on her own but she's getting used to it, getting so she can manage it quite well by herself. There have been a few close shaves, a couple of occasions she's missed something, and had to return to the airlock and repressurise it before her mistake kills her. She no longer feels any fear, she has survived all this so far, she knows she will make it home although she cannot identify the source of her confidence.

Perhaps it is Wesley.

☆

The day comes; it is time to leave. The guidance computer for the MEM ascent module has been remotely programmed by Mission Control. Anna Louise climbs the ladder from the habitation module up into the ascent module. Wesley is already in his seat, so Anna Louise seals the hatch and settles in the pilot's seat. She pulls on her communications cap and plugs the cable into the instrument panel.

I'm ready, she tells Houston. We're ready to go.

There is no point in a countdown from Mission Control, it would be eight minutes over by the time it reached her. But still she must document every action she takes on the Ascent Checklist, open to the first page, which she has strapped to one thigh of her dirty orange-smeared spacesuit.

Master arm on, she says.

Helium system pressurised, she says.

Tanks one through four are good, she says.

She confirms the guidance computer has been loaded with the correct program for the launch from the surface and rendezvous with the Mars Transfer Vehicle in Martian orbit. There is, she decides, a kind of comfort in these events, written on her checklist and then manually performed. Something could still go wrong, of course; but the act of documenting it before the fact, planning each action, makes that seem unlikely.

Anna Louise puts her finger over the Manual Engine On button, but does not push it. She glances across at Wesley, but his seat is empty. It has always been empty. His presence has enabled her to live, to survive, but she does not need him now, she is going home.

She presses the button.

Beneath her, clamps disengage with bangs that echo throughout the ascent module. Dinitrogen tetroxide and Aerozine 50 meet and mingle and explode in the combustion chamber. Anna Louise hears a distant roaring, transmitted up through the aluminium and titanium of her spacecraft, an unquenchable rumble as if a wall of Ophir Chasma were falling, collapsing, calving great mountains of red stone, to tumble and slide ten kilometres down to the chasma's floor.

But she is going up, she feels it now, acceleration pressing her into her seat. She looks across at the nearest horizon window, and she can see it, she can see the Martian horizon, red below and pink above, slowly sliding down the glass. The ascent module is shaking and rattling, the instrument panel seems to vibrate. She closes her eyes and waits patiently for it to end. Her weight is climbing, it's getting hard to breath, she's weak after so long in zero gravity and thirty days on the Martian surface, she wants the pain to end.

☆

The MTV is a line of cylinders bolted together, a pencil of white against the black, J-2 rocket engines at one end, hab module at the other, a hab module that will now be twice as roomy as it was during the trip to Mars. The MEM's guidance computer is so much smarter than that of the Apollo spacecraft—and so it should be, this close to the new millennium. Anna Louise has nothing to do but watch meters and dials as the MEM docks, as the two spacecraft come together on a television screen helpfully annotated with reticules. The docking itself she feels with a physicality she had thought lost to her, a clash of spacecraft that thuds and clangs and generates shockwaves through metal, leaving Anna Louise in no doubt as to what has just happened.

She swims through the docking tunnel from the MEM to the MTV and it doesn't feel like coming home, though she would have been surprised if it did. She turns to watch Wesley as he joins her, and she is grateful that he—no, *she*— has decided he is still needed. She does have, after all, another 430 days before she arrives in Earth orbit. Floating in the middle of the docking adaptor, she realises she has only been away thirty days but it feels like so much longer. She swims forward into the hab module and pushes off from the hatchway down to the control station in the centre of the "floor".

She buckles herself into one of the two seats, and lights on the instrument panel begin to flash and then shine steadily—Houston remotely programming the Trans Earth Injection burn and her long journey back home, swinging through the inner Solar System, slingshotting around Venus to catch up with the Earth. All she is required to do is verbally confirm the readings on the various meters, and perhaps recycle circuits if the reading is not as expected.

Houston tells her she has thirty minutes before the burn, so she releases herself from her seat and returns to the MEM ascent module. She empties it of the sample cases, sealed boxes of rock and sand, pieces of the Red Planet she is taking with her, just as Mars has taken something from her. After sealing the hatch to the MEM, she jettisons the spacecraft, and watches through a window as it tumbles silently away, propelled by the air left in the docking tunnel.

Back in the hab module, she positions herself before a horizon window. Beneath her, beneath the MTV, a red plain textured with mountains and canyons, with montes and valles, with craters, fills her view. She watches as it slides sedately past, and hangs onto a handle while the MTV thrums and clangs as the J-2 fires its TEI burn. The spacecraft shudders, continues to tremble, as Mars drifts away. She looks back over her shoulder and sees Wesley floating in the middle of the module. She gives him a wan smile, knowing she has yet to say goodbye to him.

And so the long nights travelling through the silent dark pass. Houston keeps Anna Louise busy, experiments from the storage module beyond the docking adaptor, preparation for the manoeuvre about Venus, collating the results of all the work she performed on Mars. Venus is exciting, to see it from so close a distance, she describes it excitedly to Wesley... prompting Houston to ask how she is coping. They prescribe tranquilisers, she lies and says she has swallowed them; they must know from her biometric data she hasn't, but they say nothing.

After the thrill of Venus, dull routine reasserts itself and Anna Louise knows it is time to let Wesley go. She feels something deep within her settle and slide away, like an iceberg breaking loose to slip effortlessly and soundlessly into the water and float away. Now it is time to grieve. It will make the remaining four months of the journey hard, almost impossible in fact, but she has the Earth beckoning bright and lively at the end of it.

For several days, Anna Louise feels as empty within as the universe outside the MTV. But she recovers—the routine helps, Houston and its many voices helps, the Earth growing closer each day helps. She hurtles through the void, while her heart begins to knit together the hole left in it by Wesley's disappearance. Physically, she is in poor shape, she has not felt warm since leaving Mars orbit, and though she regularly checks the environmental settings, everything seems normal. She shivers, she trembles. Her eyesight is no longer as sharp as it was, her hair is thinner, she has lost far too much weight. She suspects her fingers will never recover and she will always have disfigured nails. The sores and bruises have healed, but agonisingly slowly, and she can still feel pain from them, phantom pain perhaps.

All too soon, she's close enough to home now the signal-lag is mere seconds, small enough to hold an actual conversation. And if she directs the telescope toward the right quadrant, she can even see the Earth waiting for her. At this distance, it is a small bright dot, a blue tinge only just becoming evident.

I'm nearly home, Houston, she says.

Houston, she says again, I'm nearly home.

There is no reply.

Back to the telescope, and she peers out into space, into the lightless, lifeless dark through which she is travelling. There's the earth, but it no longer shines so brightly. It's dimming, the light fading, turning black. Now she can no longer see it, the Earth has gone.

She is alone, she has always been alone.

(with apologies to François Ozon)

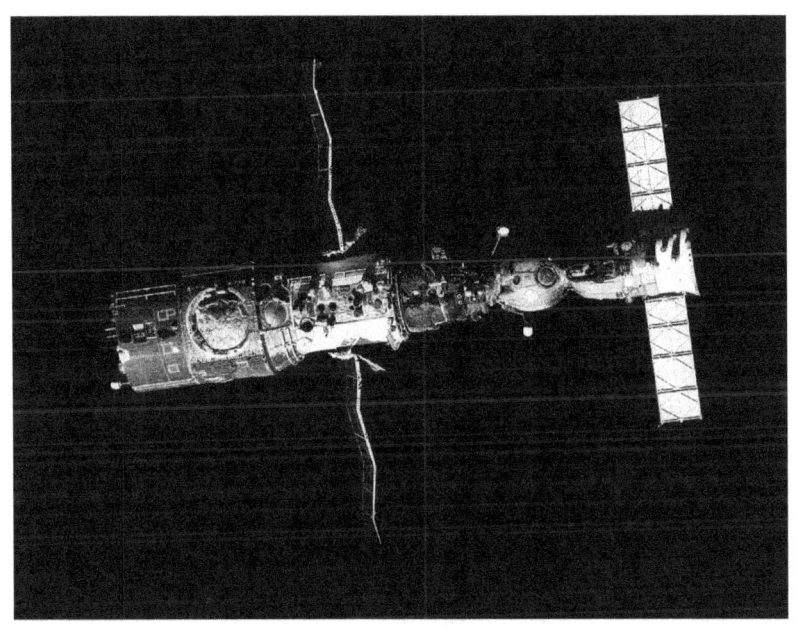

OUR GLORIOUS
SOCIALIST FUTURE
AMONG THE STARS!

Red landscape dominates the view through one of the
two tiny windows in the orbital module; it rolls
ponderously below, a rust-coloured world fleetingly
wisped with clouds, its canyons and escarpments and shield
volcanoes sharp in detail. Gagarin stares at the Red Planet,
all too aware he will see it soon from closer still. Someone
back in Moscow miscalculated, and Mars has captured the

MOK, the Martian orbital craft, on its flyby, and pulled it into orbit. A decaying orbit. The N1 stage does not have sufficient propellant remaining for a transfer injection—the spacecraft was supposed to swing about Mars and head home on a free-return trajectory.

Komarov is in the descent module, raging at the Command and Measurement Complex. But nothing can be done. They've already used up the Soyuz's DO-1 propellant, to no avail, and now the MOK is slowly spiralling toward the Martian surface. To have come so far and failed galls them both, but Gagarin is resigned to his fate.

Yuri Alekseyevich Gagarin and Vladimir Mikhaylovich Komarov will be the first men on Mars. They will not be going home afterwards.

Komarov thinks he has the MOK aligned correctly for entry into Mars' atmosphere. Gagarin leaves the Salyut in which they have lived for the past eighteen months, passes through the Soyuz orbital module and joins him in the descent module. He seals the hatch and they both strap into their moulded seats. There is a series of bangs, and the Soyuz shudders as it undocks from the Salyut and N1; and now the descent module shakes as the orbital module and equipment module are jettisoned. Gagarin looks across at Komarov, but the man is scowling fiercely at the Sirius instrument panel as if willing the spacecraft to do his bidding. Komarov has nursed a spacecraft down from orbit before. He nearly died doing it. This descent should not kill them, but it will only delay the inevitable.

They have enough supplies in the Granat-6 survival kit to last them three days on the Kazakhstani steppes. But even the deepest winter there is more hospitable than the Martian surface.

Gagarin is pressed into his seat as the descent module hits Mars' thin atmosphere and drag reduces its velocity. The window by Komarov's head glows yellow. Gagarin can feel the heat through the steel wall beside him. The Gs increase and Gagarin grunts. Komarov has miscalculated, they are going ballistic. It will be a hard landing.

It is worse, much worse, than anticipated. They hurtle across the Martian sky at more than 230 metres per second. The drogue chute, which should drop their speed to eighty metres per second, was designed for Earth, and Mars' atmosphere is far too thin, two and hundred fifty times thinner. Komarov and Gagarin will hit the ground too fast.

Stupayte s bogom, whispers Komarov.

God cannot help them now. Gagarin remains quiet. He remembers the thrill of the launch—the USSR sending men to Mars, the American space programme scrambling to catch up after its Moon landings.

The main chutes deploy but are just as ineffective as the drogue. The descent module continues to fall. Too fast.

Komarov explains they must use the landing-retros, they must use them now.

Gagarin is commander, but he has done nothing since the MOK was captured by Mars. If they can drop their speed enough, they might survive a landing. The landing-retros are designed to fire one second before hitting the ground, after the main chutes have brought the descent module's speed down to seven metres per second, down to something survivable. The landing-rockets make the touchdown more comfortable.

Poyekhali, Gagarin says.

There is a chance it might work, he thinks. Komarov is good at this, he is an engineer-pilot. Gagarin is a pilot only.

Komarov ekes out the propellant in a series of timed bursts and it seems to help. They have no way of knowing their exact velocity—the Sirius instrument panel does not feature a speedometer. But the rate of descent meter has slowed. Of course, the gravity on Mars is a third that of Earth; they could still walk away from a hard landing... Though it is scant comfort, as they will not survive for long afterwards.

The altimeter reads one thousand metres. The descent module plummets. The last of the landing-retros propellant has gone. Komarov raises a hand to his helmet in a mocking salute, and then crosses both arms over his chest. Gagarin adopts the same position. They watch the altimeter... eight hundred metres... five hundred metres... one hundred metres...

A great hand seems to swat the descent module. Something crunches and snaps beneath Gagarin's seat, and it lurches to one side. Komarov lets out a wordless yell. Gagarin cannot breathe, he wonders what is broken inside him. Such a sudden stop!

And now the module is rolling. Everything whirls about the two cosmonauts. Dizziness overwhelms Gagarin, and he struggles to keep his stomach down and his wits about him. There is a moment of quiet clarity as the module bounces into the air. Then it hits the ground again, and it's rolling and spinning and careering across the Martian sand.

Eventually it comes to rest. For several long minutes, Gagarin cannot move. Every part of his body aches, but as he tests each limb and digit, he realises nothing is broken. He gives thanks, and looks across at Komarov. They have come to rest on the module's side, and the other cosmonaut hangs in his seat higher than Gagarin. His eyes are closed and there is a look of peace on his face.

Vova, says Gagarin. Vova, my zdes.

Komarov does not reply. Gagarin undoes his straps and manages to lift his torso out of his seat, the better to see Komarov. His comrade's head, he now sees, is at an odd angle. Taking Komarov's hand, Gagarin lifts it. The man feels light, too light, as if some vital substance has leaked from his body and only the shell remains. Gagarin drops Komarov's hand. It falls limply.

Gagarin is alone. On the surface of the Red Planet.

☆

According to the academicians, the surface of Mars is an inhospitable red desert, with temperatures lower than

Siberia or Novaya Zemlya and air so thin the blood in a man's lungs would boil. Gagarin stands beside the charred descent module, and stares across a sea of rust-coloured dunes toward a great escarpment of salmon-coloured rock. He has no idea where on Mars he has landed. He turns about and scans the desert beyond the spacecraft, but he can see no mountains, no shield volcanoes. That, at least, tells him he is not on the Tharsis Bulge, not in Amazonis Planitia or Syria Planum. He looks up, where the sky fades from rose to black, the familiar constellations remind him of cold nights on the steppes back in Mother Russia, and his heart burns with homesickness.

There is nothing to see here, only the descent module and, scattered about it, rocks across which small flames dance. Before he finds somewhere to spend what little time remains to him, there is something Gagarin must do. It is a struggle to remove Komarov's body from his moulded seat inside the descent module and haul him out through the top hatch. Once he has him on the Martian sand, Gagarin rests and stares down at his comrade. To have come so far...

Komarov was made a Hero of the Soviet Union after Soyuz 1. He nursed a malfunctioning spacecraft out of orbit and into its re-entry path. No one expected him to survive, but the chutes opened as designed, the landing-retros fired, and the Soyuz 1 descent module hit the black earth of Mother Russia as if nothing had gone wrong. Komarov had been an angry bear in the days following, uncompromising in his disgust over the shoddy workmanship on the spacecraft. He took charge of redesigning and re-engineering everything. There was no other man Gagarin could have chosen to accompany him on his flyby of Mars.

And now, neither of them will ever leave.

After he has buried Komarov in the cold red sand, Gagarin slings the survival kit over his shoulder and sets out toward the cliff. He does not know how far away it is— he has no way to judge its size. The horizon is closer than Earth's, so it cannot be more than a kilometre or two from the descent module.

The Yastreb spacesuit was designed to keep its wearer cool in the vacuum of space, but the surface of Mars has enough of an atmosphere to convect away heat. As he trudges across the fine red desert Gagarin begins to chill. The backpack threatens to unbalance him and he must lean further forward than is comfortable. The light gravity helps, however—he weighs only some forty kilos, even in the spacesuit. He looks up through the visor of his helmet but the cliff appears no closer. The Yastreb's backpack has sufficient air for 150, perhaps 180, minutes. He stumbles on, blind to his surroundings, focused only on the wall of rock ahead. He mutters prayers under his breath, tries to remember his childhood on the collective farm in Klushino before the Great Patriotic War. He must think pleasant thoughts, be determined, be like steel; or he might as well have lay down beside Vova.

The ground beneath his boots changes. It is no longer slippery sand but a dusting of fine grains upon rock. He looks up and sees he is no more than twenty metres from the foot of the cliff. He remembers nothing of the past thirty minutes, of putting one foot before the other. His shoulders ache from the backpack and the survival kit, his feet are sore, and the Yastreb has rubbed him raw on hips and neck. He rests a moment at the foot of the cliff. Looking back across the desert, he can see his footsteps through the sand and the dust devils which whirl above them. In the distance, he can make out a black dot in the rust-red, drawing the eye: the descent module. He turns and looks up at the rock-face. It must be hundreds of metres high, perhaps even a kilometre. He has never seen so tall and so sheer a cliff before. It is impossible to climb, but he will not succumb to despair. He is tired, in pain, cold, and he feels enclosed and claustrophobic in the Yastreb's helmet. He puts out a hand, as if to feel the world before him, but can touch nothing through the layers of his glove. It does not matter—he will not be here long.

But should anyone else ever visit Mars, they will know the Soviet Union was here first.

☆

He walks along the foot of the escarpment until he finds a break in the rock. It is a vertical fracture some three metres wide, with a small ramp of rubble at its foot. Gagarin clambers up the pile of stone—it is so old it has settled and is as hard as concrete. He sees the ramp has slid the entire depth of the fracture, forming a slope upwards between sheer walls. Perhaps he will find somewhere up there to lay down for his final rest, perhaps he will find a route to the top of this cliff. There is nothing for him here at its foot. He begins the steep walk up the fracture.

Within ten minutes, he regrets his decision. His thighs and calves burn, and his ankles are even more sore than before. But still he struggles onward. The rift opens out into a small flat area like the bottom of a deep well. He looks up and high above can see the small rose-coloured circle that is the sky. There are cracks in the walls around him, and one looks wide enough to be the entrance to something deeper. He stumbles across to it and pokes his head and shoulders inside. There is enough light for him to see that it is a small cave some five metres deep and four metres wide. Brightness glints from the back wall, so he enters and moves toward it. Rubbing one gloved hand against the rock, he uncovers a seam of ice, a thick jagged line of blue-white stitched into the red.

Water.

He will not go thirsty at least. He has enough food in the Granat-6 to last him a week, perhaps longer if he rations himself. But he has only around an hour's worth of oxygen left in his backpack. If he returns to the descent module and fetches Komarov's backpack—a walk there of almost an hour, and the same back—then he might have an extra two hours before he asphyxiates. Even a man desperate to survive can see the futility of such a trip. Gagarin cannot live here without his spacesuit: the surface pressure is less than one percent of Earth's, with only trace amounts of oxygen. Sitting down, he leans back against the cave-wall with its streak of ice and thinks to himself he has chosen a fine tomb. It is a good size this cave, with smooth walls and a floor mostly clear of rubble or detritus. There is even a flat shelf of rock to one side—an excellent place in which to lie in state. He can see himself there already, on his back, arms crossed over his chest, his helmet visor... Open? Or closed?

Visor open, his body will freeze quicker and be better preserved for the ages. He is fairly sure the low temperature will mummify him, though he is not an expert. He is a pilot, a cosmonaut, not a doctor or academician. A thought occurs to him. While he is confident his body will be discovered one day, that the history books will show—not for many centuries perhaps—he was both the first human being into space and the first human being on Mars... It strikes him that his body may prove unidentifiable, his features mummified beyond recognition, the name stitched onto his Yastreb perhaps unreadable. So he reaches for the Granat-6 survival kit and from it pulls out the folding knife. He will carve his name in the rock above the shelf, he will write his own epitaph. If the exertion hastens his demise, so be it. At least he will never be forgotten.

It takes him thirty minutes before he is satisfied with his handiwork. On a flat stretch of cave-wall directly above the rock shelf, he has carved his name: Юрий Алексéевич Гагáрин. Beneath it, he adds: для Родина-Мать, for the Motherland. And then the date.

Now all he can do is wait for the end.

☆

Yuri Gagarin was not the first man in space because he gave up, he was not made commander of the first fly-by mission of Mars because he refused to fight for what he wanted. So why, he asks himself, has he resigned himself to his imminent death? True, it seems unavoidable. There is nothing he can do, he cannot magic oxygen out of... thin air. The thought prompts a smile, but it does not alter his situation. He refuses to surrender to despair, he will only lie down moments before the end. He wraps his arms about his chest. Though he is used to the cold—he is Russian, after all—he is suffering from the chill, and he wishes for a fire. He imagines blazing logs in the centre of the cave's floor, giving out welcome heat, making of the cave a warm and cosy khata. And then he remembers seeing rocks scattered about the descent module out on the desert, rocks which were *burning*.

There is not enough oxygen on Mars for fire. How could the stones be alight? Perhaps they *contain* oxygen? He considers whether it is worth investigating. He has enough oxygen for the walk back to the descent module, and he can then switch over to Komarov's unused backpack... But is he merely delaying the inevitable, or could it be a real chance for survival?

He has no choice. Gagarin rises to his feet. A chance at survival, no matter how slim, or how short an extension on life if it gives him, must be taken. After all, are not the Soviet cosmonauts "the pioneers of the universe"?

He leaves the survival kit in the cave, and begins the long trek back to the descent module. This time, the walk is harder—he is tired, his bones ache from the cold, and though he recognises that wishful thinking is driving him, he is determined not to fail. He arrives at the edge of the desert and gazes out across wave after wave of copper-coloured sand. There is a line of footprints leading the way to the small black dot of the descent module, though the footprints are blurred where wind devils have run back and forth across them. Gagarin trudges forward, propelled by hope, knowing that even if the burning rocks are nothing but a figment of his imagination, he will still have Komarov's backpack. That will get him back to the cave, that will give him time to make his peace.

And then he looks up and the charred bucket-shape of the MOK's descent module is no more than twenty metres ahead, and something flickers to the left and the right and before it. As he nears, he sees with rising spirits they are guttering flames... issuing from small rocks and stones. How is this possible? He increases his pace, stumbling through the red sand, hoping he is not victim to a mirage. But no, he picks up a large rock, perhaps a kilo in weight and ten cubic centimetres in volume, and there is plainly a flame issuing from its top. He looks closer—the rock is porous and appears to contain tiny lacunae.

Gagarin is no geologist, he does not know if stone can hold pockets of oxygen, even on this new world. But he cannot discount the evidence of his eyes. It is fated—they call this world the Red Planet, the left breast of Gagarin's spacesuit bears the Red Star. It was not a miscalculation which sent Komarov and Gagarin plummeting to the surface of Mars, it was the hand of socialist destiny.

After he has changed over to Komarov's backpack, and verified it contains 180 minutes of oxygen, he fashions a rough sled from the descent module's top hatch, and on it he places his own backpack and as many of the burning rocks as he can find scattered about. It is a struggle to get the sled moving over the sand, even though its contents weigh only a fraction of what they would on Earth. Using the straps from his backpack as a yoke, he curses his way back across the desert toward the red cliffs.

Gagarin has delayed the inevitable but he has not defeated it. Thanks to the burning rocks, the seam of ice in the cave wall, and the rations in the Granat-6 he will live a few days longer, perhaps a week or two. Of course, there is no way a rescue mission could reach him during that time—even if the USSR had the technology to land on, and then launch from, the Martian surface. If they were to launch supplies aboard a probe, it would be months, perhaps years, before it arrived. It is all moot, he has no way to contact the Command and Measurement Complex; they probably think he is dead, and they would not be wrong to think so.

He sits in his cave, wearing his spacesuit, visor closed. After some experimentation, he manages to fashion a crude device from the heat exchanger in his backpack which will hold a handful of small burning rocks. He uses one of the tubes which normally carries oxygen from the backpack to the spacesuit to pipe oxygen from the rocks directly into his helmet. A kilo of rocks provides enough oxygen to last four hours, providing he breathes shallowly and does not exert himself. Despite the flames, the oxygen is cold and the fire gives off no heat. For the time-being, this will suffice—it will at least mean he has sufficient oxygen to return to the crash site and collect more rocks.

That first night on Mars, he comes close to freezing to death. He is tired and cold and he never has enough air, but he does not die. In the morning when he wakes, his body aches, his hands shake, his lungs hurt; but he knows he has beaten the Red Planet for the moment. He sucks some ice, it is so cold it pains his teeth, and then chews on some rations.

Over the course of several days, he strips the descent module of its contents and drags them on his sled to the cave. He learns that powdering the rocks releases the oxygen stored in its lacunae all at once. He jury-rigs a device from his backpack's internal workings which he can refresh with powdered rock and which, through a filter, will provide him with breathable oxygen.

On one of his explorations of the area surrounding his cave, he finds a sheet of ice threaded with branching black lines. It is like nothing he has seen before. He hacks into the ice with the machete from the survival kit, and a black substance pours in thin lines from capillaries within the frozen water. It appears to have a glutinous texture and he realises with some shock it is organic. It is life, Martian life. A lichen or an algae, he is no biologist or botanist. He wonders if he can eat it; then he realises he has no choice, he must try.

Now that he has found one sheet of ice with black threads—he calls it ikra, "caviar", a black joke—he seems to find it everywhere. The walls of the canyon are riddled with it. He uses the glass cover of the navigation indicator from the descent module's Sirius instrument panel, and fills it with ikra. Back at the cave, he sits and stares at the black goo and knows it will be either his salvation or his death. He picks up the glass dish, raises his visor, winces as the cold strikes his face, and slowly tips the ikra into his mouth. It tastes metallic and has the texture of mucus. He gags but he is not sick. He waits, he can feel it sitting in his stomach, there is a twinge, a slight acid reflux, but he swallows repeatedly and he thinks he might be all right.

Gagarin wakes during the night in a cold sweat. The padding inside his helmet is icy and damp, and his stomach burns. He curls up and tries to will the poison from his body. Eventually, he falls asleep again. When he wakes again, it is daylight, the cave opening glowing faintly from the weak sunlight which reaches the bottom of the crevasse. He rises gingerly to his feet and is surprised to discover he feels fine. No, he feels *invigorated*. Whatever was in the ikra, it seems to have done him good. He feels better than he has done for days—he does not ache, his lungs do not hurt, his throat is not sore, his sinuses do not feel as though they have been scraped clean with sandpaper.

Bozhe moy, he says in wonder.

Two weeks after he crashed on Mars, Gagarin has lost

weight, his stocky body is weak and thin, but he is still alive. He spends his days exploring the canyon, hunting for a source of oxygen rocks closer than the red desert. At the top of the cliff is a rocky plateau, which descends in a gentle slope to a plain of fractured rocks in brown and umber and red. Beyond it are hills, striped with grey and salmon and black. At the horizon, the sky rises through shades of rose and pink to black at the zenith. He turns about and now he looks over an ocean of red sand, stretching as far as he can see, endless waves of pale crimson, fading into the sky. This is his world, this is his Red Planet.

He is Gagarin of Mars.

He walks along the parapet searching for oxygen rocks. Like the water ice and the ikra, they are relatively common; but now he has to range further afield to find them. He has yet to find any "socialist vegetation" or any of the small rodents imagined by Klushantev, but this does not surprise him. Mars is dead. Down on the plain, he hunts among boulders for the telltale sponge-like rocks, but his eye is caught by a pile of stones in the centre of a small open area—it seems too regular a shape to have formed naturally. It looks like a cairn, some three metres in length, two metres in width and two metres high. Puzzled, he crosses to it and begins to remove the stones.

There is something hidden among the rocks. He digs for it, pushing stones to either side as if swimming through rubble.

A hands falls out.

Gagarin straightens in shock. It is a human hand, four fingers and a thumb, blackened and shrunk by cold. It is impossible.

He is not the first human being on Mars.

Someone beat him to it. No, at least two people. Someone must have built this cairn. Who? The Americans? How? The USSR has been leading the Space Race since the launch of Sputnik I in 1957.

Urgently, he pulls rocks from the cairn, until he has uncovered the body of a human male. He is tall and thin, with shoulder-length black hair, and is clad only in a short black kilt of some rubber-like material.

If there are people on Mars, where do they live? Gagarin has explored the area surrounding his cave, although no more than a kilometre's distance in each direction. He has found no evidence of life, nothing but the algae-like organism he calls ikra and on which he lives. No Toscoob and the Atlanteans he ruled, no communist utopia as imagined by Bogdanov, not even the canals described by Kazantsev... The academicians had it right: Mars is a dead world. During his world tour following his Vostok 1 flight, Gagarin saw some of the American fantasies set on Mars, but he had thought them no less fanciful than the utopian dreams of Bogdanov and Tolstoi. The reality is this, a red desert with air so thin he must live permanently in his Yastreb, and a mean surface temperature lower than that of the worst winter on Novaya Zemlya. This body he has found, it must be a visitor.

Gagarin sits on a nearby boulder and contemplates the corpse. Though he has been here only fourteen days and, if he were brutally honest, he cannot really expect to survive more than a week or two longer... The irka sustains him, but the cold eats away at him and he shivers almost constantly; and always being on the edge of breathlessness weakens him with each passing day. He has always thought he would have time to build some sort of monument for himself and Komarov, a message to the ages, something to tell the future that the USSR was first to land on the Red Planet.

But now he knows he was not the first.

☆

It is getting late. Night begins to fall, a slow leaching of colour from a peach sky, so Gagarin quickly rebuilds the cairn, re-interring the body, and says a brief prayer over the grave. As he turns to make his way home, a paleness on the horizon catches his attention. He squints, he reaches up a glove to wipe dust from his helmet's visor. There is a dome of light crowning the line of hills some two kilometres away on the other side of the plain. Yellow and plainly artificial light. How has he not spotted it before?

Gagarin checks his oxygen supply and judges he has at least two hours left. The cave is a fifteen-minute hike away. The hills are much further, perhaps a forty-minute walk, even in Mars' lighter gravity. He has enough oxygen to investigate, and he cannot afford to not do so, even though it will be the furthest distance from his cave Gagarin has walked on the Red Planet. He has no idea what lies beyond the hills, but there is only one way he will find out.

Fortunately, the ground is mostly flat, and inclines gently away from him. He starts forward, picking his way carefully, avoiding the scattered rocks and the narrow rills which snake across the landscape. It takes him half an hour to reach the hills, and then he must climb them; but the stone is friable and breaks easily in his gloved hands when he tries to pull himself up the slope. He struggles upwards, by the time he reaches the top he is panting heavily and he hopes he has enough oxygen remaining for the walk back to his cave. The hills, thankfully, are not high, no more than two hundred metres, and prove to be the rim around a crater. He twists and looks back over the route he has walked. Now that he knows, he can see the jumbled rocks and stones scattered across the plain as ejecta. As he turns back to look up at the ridge five metres above him, he sees the dome of light increase in intensity. He drops onto his stomach and lies flat. After two weeks, his white Yastreb spacesuit is so smeared with red and umber and ochre it is almost camouflaged. Gagarin snakes his way to the ridge, and cautiously peers over it...

In the centre of the crater, approximately five hundred metres away, a group of people are attacking the ground with picks. They are all male, brown-skinned and wearing nothing but a short black kilt. Overseeing them are three figures in metallic spacesuits with bucket-like helmets. To one side, crouched menacingly on jointed legs, is some sort of spacecraft. It resembles nothing Gagarin has ever seen before—tall, built of cylinders one atop the other, like something from an industrial plant, and far larger than anything Earth has ever managed to lift into orbit. He is reminded of one of the spaceships from an East German movie a comrade cosmonaut once insisted he watch. He thought it silly and was surprised a man who was training to go into space aboard a Soyuz, a <u>real</u> spacecraft, should hold such fantasies in high regard.

But the sight below him is no fantasy. As he watches, one of the spacesuited figures—perhaps it is a robot, although it moves too fluidly to be mechanical—steps forward, takes something from its belt and lashes out at one of the semi-nude men. There is a flash and the man falls writhing to the floor. The other men redouble their frantic digging.

They are slaves, Gagarin realises. The digging men have been enslaved by those in the silver spacesuits. He is immediately offended. Did Lenin not say that slavery is no different to feudalism? Russia freed its serfs more than one hundred years ago—although it took socialism to truly emancipate the peasants. Gagarin knows this because he was born on a collective farm in the Smolensk oblast. He was born a peasant—and now he is a colonel in the Soviet Air Forces, a cosmonaut... and a resident of Mars.

He has seen enough. He slides back down the hill a few metres and then carefully scrambles to his feet. His descent is much faster than his ascent, this low gravity means he can make prodigious leaps, though he must take care not to land on a rock and twist his ankle. Once back on level ground, he heads east, toward the escarpment overlooking the desert, and his cave.

There is no possibility of rescue in the crater. Gagarin

does not know if the figures in spacesuits are even human, though the slaves certainly looked like men of Earth. But they could breath the thin air of Mars; and they were not affected by the cold.

☆

During the next three days, Gagarin revisits the crater and spies on the slaves and their overseers. He spends an hour each twilight, watching from the shadows as the slaves dig a deeper and deeper hole in the Martian soil. He does not know if they are mining, or unearthing something buried.

On the fourth day, one of the slaves escapes.

He must have seen Gagarin hiding in the darkness because he makes straight for him. He runs across the crater, weaving from side to side, as the overseers fire beams of light at him. None hit. At the crater's edge, the slave clambers up the slope and then dives over the ridge and into the darkness. The overseers gather together and a conversation involving terse gestures takes place. Gagarin scrambles back from his vantage point. As he works his way down the slope, a figure looms out of the night. The slave grabs Gagarin's helmet in both hands and puts his face close to the visor. He stares into Gagarin's eyes, then abruptly lets go and steps back.

Gagarin gestures for the man to follow him, and he leads him across the plain and down into the fracture which leads to his cave. Once inside the cave, Gagarin sits down on the rock-shelf and gazes at the escaped slave. They cannot speak—the Martian atmosphere is too thin to carry sounds which can be heard by the human ear. So they stare at each other.

The slave digs into a pouch hung from a belt about his waist and removes a small shiny capsule. He mimes swallowing the pill, and then pretends to take great breaths, sucking in his stomach and lifting his ribcage... He swallows the capsule, and the inhales and exhales vigorously. He takes another capsule from the pouch and holds it out to Gagarin.

The slave's meaning is clear: somehow the pill is responsible for his ability to breathe the thin atmosphere of Mars. Gagarin holds out his hand and the slave drops the pill into his gloved palm. It is a purplish colour, semi-transparent and just visible in its depths are curled and complex shapes. It does not look like any medicine Gagarin has ever seen.

The slave gestures eagerly that he should swallow the pill. Gagarin's days on Mars are numbered—though he has found local sources for oxygen, water and food, his diet cannot sustain him, the cold saps his energy every moment of the day, and he must carefully control his breathing to eke out his limited oxygen. The alien pill at least will solve one of those problems... If it works. Though the slave looks human, his internal physiology, his body chemistry, may well prove completely alien. Gagarin knows he has little choice. He must at least try.

He lifts his visor, the cold claws at his face and he immediately feels breathless. He pops the capsule into his mouth, and swallows. Moments later, he feels a warmth spread from his stomach up his chest. His lungs feel as though they are on fire, but there is no pain. He opens his mouth and without thinking sucks in a breath. He does not choke! He can breathe Mars' atmosphere! What miracle is this?

He no longer feels the knife-sharp cold against his cheeks, if he opens his mouth the moisture no longer boils from his tongue, his eyes do not feel like they are drying in their sockets. He grins at the slave. They still cannot talk, so Gagarin gestures his gratitude. Using the machete, he writes his thanks in the dirt of the cave floor, спасибо.

He follows this with his name, Юрий, and points to himself. He speaks his name, though he makes no sound of course. He offers the machete to the alien and indicates he is to identify himself in writing. The man grasps the idea immediately, and writes a line of strange symbols across the cave-floor. To Gagarin, it looks more like an equation than a name, and he guesses that spoken it would prove a mouthful. Mindful of his situation, and that this man not of Earth is now his comrade, Gagarin writes on the floor, пятница.

Pyatnitsa, he says soundlessly; and he points at the man he has named for a character from the first ever 3D feature film—yet another great Soviet achievement.

☆

The two of them spend their time spying on the overseers and the slaves, but Gagarin still cannot figure their purpose, nor can Pyatnitsa explain it to him. When not at the crater, they hunt for oxygen rocks and iksa. One morning, Pyatnitsa disappears and returns several hours later with several sheets of slick plastic-like material. He must have stolen them from his comrades at the crater. Using the fabric, Pyatnitsa constructs a crude airlock over the entrance to the cave. Gagarin finds the material fascinating. When struck sharply, with a rock or the handle of the machete, it becomes stiff and inflexible like a sheet of good Soviet steel. But a gentle stroking movement with the fingers returns it to a fabric. Once the cave is sealed, the two of them powder oxygen rocks until there is sufficient pressure to carry sound.

And so the language lessons begin...

Given Pyatnitsa's native name, Gagarin thinks it best to teach his comrade Russian. The vocabulary comes easily enough—tovarishch, kamen, led, iksa, skafandr, nosimyi avariynyi, zapas... But Pyatnitsa is soon lost among the complexities of Russian grammar. He uses his own alien tongue to demonstrate—through a combination of diagrams sketched on the cave-floor with a finger, gestures and spoken word he explains that his language possesses only sixteen simple grammatical rules. It is easier, Gagarin reluctantly admits to himself, that he learn Pyatnitsa's language. And so he does. The first words he learns are: koo, a general interrogative; and kyu, a profanity.

Within a week, they can converse reasonably well. Outside, on the Martian surface, they must use gestures and hand-signals, but once through the airlock and inside the cave, they can speak normally. The magical alien pill still allows Gagarin to breathe the Martian atmosphere and protects him from the chill. He continues to wear his spacesuit, and the helmet is useful for protecting him against the UV; but now he keeps the visor up—and his vision is much improved, as it is no longer blurred and obscured by dusty polycarbonate.

Pyatnitsa—he accepts the name gratefully, as his own is merely a number given him at birth by the Engineers, as he calls the overseers; he explains it is the fourth symbol of his people's syllabary, which he follows with an open hand twice and then a hand with two fingers folded in—Pyatnitsa tells Gagarin that a long time ago a powerful spaceship from Centuria crashed on the Red Planet, and the Engineers believe this is the origin of the crater. They will keep on digging until they find it... if it is truly there to be found. Then they will return to the Andromeda Nebula and use the wrecked spaceship to build more powerful spaceships of their own.

The Martian days pass and Gagarin broods. In Pyatnitsa he has found a worthy comrade, who may very well have saved his life with his magical pill; but the man is woefully ignorant of political realities. To him, slavery is a natural condition, and when Gagarin explains socialism, Pyatnitsa has trouble grasping the concept. In his society, there is no equality, there is no dignity, there is nothing but what the Engineers say. Pyatnitsa was born a slave and he will die a slave. Or he would have, had he not seen Gagarin hiding in the shadows.

Socialism, Gagarin tells Pyatnitsa, is the future of

mankind, this is self-evident through historical materialism. As it has superseded capitalism, so it will lead to world communism, to a human utopia.

Capitalism, Gagarin says, is slavery—Pyatnitsa's people may be owned by the Engineers, but so too are the Engineers owned by their capitalist system. In a communist society, the means of production are owned by the workers. Each produces according to his ability, and this is available to each according to his needs.

Pyatnitsa sits on the cave floor, legs crossed and chin on hands, and gazes at Gagarin in admiration.

History is a process, Gagarin explains; societies undergo several stages on the path to political enlightenment. Marx identified five such stages: primitive communism, slavery—the Engineers and Pyatnitsa's people are at this stage!—feudalism, capitalism and socialism. But history has also indicated a sixth stage exists: communism. The West—and this requires a further explanation of Earth's geopolitics by Gagarin—is capitalistic, and so it is a "neurotic society". The USSR, a socialist nation, is leading Earth's nations into the future. Gagarin's mission to Mars was just one of many Soviet technological achievements, which stand as testament to the Soviet pioneering spirit.

He continues, The communists are the most advanced and resolute section of the working class of every country, the section which pushes forward all others. Their aim is the formation of the proletariat into a class, overthrow of the bourgeois supremacy, and conquest of political power by the proletariat. In a communist society, accumulated labour is a means to widen, to enrich, to promote the existence of the labourer.

Perhaps, suggests Pyatnitsa, Gagarin can show this communism to his people?

I consider it my duty to do so, Gagarin replies. They must cast off the yoke of slavery, he says; they must overthrow the Engineers.

The Engineers will kill them, says Pyatnitsa.

Some will die, Gagarin admits. But blood must be shed for the sake of a better future. They will not do it on their own: the great honour of beginning the revolution must fall to us.

☆

Gagarin bounds down from the ridge of the crater, taking great leaps in the one-third gravity. The slaves are deep in the hole they are digging, and the Engineers' attention is focused on them. Gagarin makes no noise, though he throws up great clouds of ochre dust. One of the Engineers seems to sense his approach and turns toward him—

Gagarin tackles the creature about the middle and they both tumble to the red dirt. He holds a rock he has carefully shaped over the past week into rough point. Using both hands, he hammers at the strip of black glass on the Engineer's helmet which serves as a visor. Pyatnitsa, he sees, has taken a pick from somewhere and is swinging it at another Engineer.

The visor silently shatters, and the Engineer beneath Gagarin shudders and then goes still. He pushes the body into the pit dug by the slaves, and then rolls to one side as an Engineer fires its weapon at him. Scrambling to his feet, Gagarin launches himself at another target. He flies through the thin air... and collides with the Engineer. Once again, Gagarin's rock smashes the visor, and the Engineer lies still.

Gagarin rises to his feet and turns. Pyatnitsa is at the top of the ramp leading down into the pit, gesturing urgently for the slaves to join him. Gagarin grins. The struggle has begun, this is revolution. Blood will flow on the Red Planet; in a manner of speaking, this is the *third* Martian invasion.

There are so many more slaves than Gagarin realised, forty, fifty, perhaps even more. And they are all armed with picks. The three Engineers who had been overseeing them are now dead, but more must remain in their great

106

spacecraft. One of Pyatnitsa's people steps forward and makes a gesture of respect to Gagarin, and then reverently hands him a pick. Gagarin wants to say something but of course the air is too thin to carry sound. Instead, he makes a fist, raises it, and then points at the Engineers' vessel. The slaves raise their own fists and their mouths gape in a soundless cheer.

Gagarin leads his rebels toward the enemy spaceship. A ramp between two of the landing legs leads up to an open hatchway. He rushes up the ramp and inside. As soon as he steps over the threshold, he hears sound, a fatherly murmur, and feels warmth—there is some sort of invisible wall preventing the atmosphere within the alien vessel from escaping. Turning to Pyatnitsa and the freed slaves, he gestures for them to follow him.

Poyekhali!, he shouts.

Pick held high, he runs along the corridor. An Engineer steps from a doorway and into Gagarin's path. Gagarin swings his pick with both hands, it sinks into the creature's bucket helmet, and the figure jerks and goes limp. Pulling his weapon free, Gagarin turns and shouts:

Workers of Mars, unite!

You have nothing to lose but your chains!

You have a galaxy to win!

ACKNOWLEDGEMENTS

'Barker' originally appeared in British Fantasy Society
Journal, Winter 2010

'Faith' originally appeared in The Maginot Line, Rob
Redman, ed., April 2012

'The Spaceman and the Moon Girl' originally appeared in
Litro Magazine #137, August 2014

'The Incurable Irony of the Man Who Rode the Rocket
Sled' originally appeared in The Orphan 3, July 2013

'Far Voyager' originally appeared in Postscripts 32/33
Far Voyager, Nick Gevers, ed., November 2014

'Red Desert' originally appeared in Space-Houston We
Have a Problem, Alex Davies, ed., January 2016

'Our Glorious Socialist Future Among the Stars!' is
original to this collection

PHOTO CREDITS

page 9: Little Joe 5, unmanned atmospheric test of Mercury spacecraft, 8 Nov 1960 – photo credit: NASA

page 23: Yuri Gagarin inside Vostok 1 – photo credit Footagevault

page 33: One of Paco Rabanne's "Twelve Unwearable Dresses in Contemporary Materials", 1966 – photo credit: Life Magazine

page 39: Typical set-up on the Gee Whiz rocket sled, date unknown – photo credit: Edwards Air Force Base History Office

page 51: Skylab space station – photo credit: NASA

page 65: Curiosity's tyre-tracks after it crossed the "Dingo Gap" sand dune, 9 Feb 2014 – photo credit: NASA

page 85: Salyut 6 and Soyuz 36 (Expedition 5), May 1980 – photo credit: unknown (presumably Sergei Korolev's OKB-1)

ABOUT THE AUTHOR

Ian Sales wanted to be an astronaut when he grew up, but sadly wasn't born in the USA or USSR. So he writes about them instead. He also owns a large number of books on the subject. Ian has had fiction published in a number of science fiction and literary magazines and has appeared in several anthologies. In 2012, he edited the anthology *Rocket Science* for Mutation Press. In 2013, he won the BSFA Award for *Adrift on the Sea of Rains*, the first book of the Apollo Quartet, and was nominated for the Sidewise Award for the same work. He has also written the remaining three books of the quartet, *The Eye With Which The Universe Beholds Itself*, *Then Will The Great Wash Deep Above* and *All That Outer Space Allows* (also published by Whippleshield Books), and a space opera trilogy, *A Prospect of War*, *A Conflict of Orders* and *A Want of Reason* (published by Tickety Boo Press). He reviews books for *Interzone*, and is represented by the John Jarrold Literary Agency. You can find him online at www.iansales.com and on Twitter as @ian_sales.

ALSO BY WHIPPLESHIELD BOOKS

The Apollo Quartet, Ian Sales

1 Adrift on the Sea of Rains (2012)
- paperback   £4.99 / $7.50 / €6.00
- ebook: PDF, EPUB, MOBI   £2.99 / $3.99 / €2.99

2 The Eye With Which The Universe Beholds Itself (2012)
- paperback   £4.99 / $7.50 / €6.00
- signed numbered hardback   £6.99 / $12.00 / €8.50
- ebook: PDF, EPUB, MOBI   £2.99 / $3.99 / €2.99

3 Then Will The Great Ocean Wash Deep Above (2013)
- paperback   £4.99 / $6.50 / €6.00
- signed numbered hardback   £6.99 / $10.00 / €8.50
- ebook: PDF, EPUB, MOBI   £2.99 / $3.99 / €2.99

4 All That Outer Space Allows (2015)
- paperback   £7.99 / $9.50 / €9.00
- signed numbered hardback   £9.99 / $13.00 / €11.50
- ebook: PDF, EPUB, MOBI   £2.99 / $3.99 / €2.99

Aphrodite Terra, edited by Ian Sales

- paperback   £4.99 / $6.50 / €6.00
- ebook: PDF, EPUB, MOBI   £2.99 / $3.99 / €2.99